CONFESSIONS of a TEENAGE LEPER

CONFESSIONS of a TEENAGE LEPER

ASHLEY LITTLE

PENGUIN TEEN
an imprint of Penguin Random House Canada Young Readers,
a Penguin Random House Company

First published 2018

1 2 3 4 5 6 7 8 9 10 (LSC)

Manufactured in the U.S.A.

Library and Archives Canada Cataloguing in Publication
Little, Ashley, 1983–, author
Confessions of a teenage leper / Ashley Little.
Issued in print and electronic formats.
ISBN 978-0-7352-6261-4 (hardcover). —ISBN 978-0-7352-6262-1 (EPUB)

I. Title.

PS8623.I898C66 2018   C813'.6   C2017-905752-9
                                           C2017-905753-7
Library of Congress Control Number: 2017960301

Text and jacket design by Five Seventeen
Edited by Samantha Swenson

www.penguinrandomhouse.ca

Penguin
Random House
PENGUIN TEEN CANADA

For Ben Parker, with thanks

They think I got it from an armadillo. Isn't that the most fucked-up thing you've ever heard? I mean, seriously. It's the twenty-first century. Who gets leprosy anymore? No one. That's who. Unless you, like, live in a gutter covered in filth or were in the Bible, or unless you're me. My name is Abby Furlowe*. I'm seventeen years old. I live in ███████, Texas. I'm blanking out the name of my town because I don't need some jerk-off coming to find me, getting all up in my face and spray-painting the words DIRTY LEPER across the front of my house. Privacy is important to me now. It didn't used to be. I used to want to model for *Seventeen* magazine. I used to want to be an A-list actress and have a beach house in Malibu. I used to fantasize about the paparazzi following me around and me blowing kisses into their cameras, or giving them the finger, depending on my mood that day. When I was a little kid, people would ask me what I wanted to be when I grew up, and I'd say, "I want to be beautiful." And then they'd laugh and say something cheesy like, "Oh, sweetie. You already *are* beautiful." And it was

----

* Not my real name

1

true. I was. I really, really was. And I wasn't one of those bleach-blonde chicks who thinks she's so pretty she could maybe be a model one day; I actually *was* that pretty. And I'm a natural blonde. I was crowned princess of my junior high, I was on the high school cheerleading squad, and I was crowned Miss ▮▮▮▮▮▮ two years ago. I got to wear a rhinestone tiara and a dress Miss Universe herself would've killed for. I stood in the back of a red convertible cruising down Main Street, waving to onlookers at the Fourth of July Parade. You would never think that now, if you saw me today, but it's true.

I guess the very first thing I noticed was a little reddish spot on my thigh, like a little sunburn patch or something. It was the summer I turned seventeen, and I was a lifeguard at the local pool. No big deal, right? It'll go away. *Just leave it alone*, I thought. But it didn't go away. That's the thing. That's the worst thing. It never really went away.

So, anyway. I waited and waited for it to go away and it didn't, so finally I showed my mom. She ran her fingers over it and poked at it, but it didn't hurt, and she squinched up her face at me like she does when she's worried about something but doesn't want to say what it is.

"*What?*" I said.

"Don't pick at it," she said.

"I haven't been picking it, Mom!"

"Okay." She nodded. "That's good."

She put some ointment on it and took me to the doctor the next day.

Dr. Jamieson was the doctor who had delivered me. He knew my complete medical history from minute one, even before that, actually, if you want to get technical. He knew about every rash, flu and infection I'd ever had. He didn't know anything about this red spot though. He thought it was eczema so he gave me a prescription for some cream. So off I went, bought the cream, put it on, blah blah blah. It didn't work. In fact, I got another little scaly patch on the side of my foot and then one on my face. On my face! Right between my eyebrows. Like, the worst possible spot, obviously. So . . . yeah. I went back to see Dr. Jamieson.

"Are they itchy?" he asked.

"Kind of." I scratched the one on my foot.

"Ringworm," he said.

"Gross!"

"It's not actually a worm," he said. "It's a fungus that lives on the skin."

"Still gross."

He whipped out his prescription pad and scribbled something illegible on it. "Should go away in two to three weeks," he said. He tore the sheet off and held it out to me, his mouth a thin, tight line.

I grabbed it and left the room, disgusted that I had a fungus. Now, I *wish* I had a fungus. I'd *welcome* a fungus.

I put the antifungal cream on all the spots every night for three weeks. The spots didn't go away. Then, when I woke up in the morning, my face would be puffy and red and my eyes all swollen up. The swelling would go down in a few hours so at least I looked okay by the time I got to the pool. It would happen the next morning, and then not for a day or two. Then it would happen again. I went back to see Dr. Jamieson.

"Could it be from something I'm eating?" I asked.

"Possibly," he said. "Let's try you on an elimination diet."

"Is that when you have to stop eating everything that tastes good?"

"Pretty much, yeah," he said.

So I cut out eggs, dairy, soy, wheat, gluten, oats, corn, citrus fruits, nightshade vegetables (tomatoes, eggplant, potatoes), nuts, seeds, caffeine, all processed foods and, hardest of all, sugar and chocolate. Basically, I ate celery, cucumbers, fish, turkey and rice for four weeks. It sucked. Nothing changed. I still got the morning puffies. I still had the spots. And they looked angry. I went back to Dr. Jamieson.

He didn't know anything. He sent me to see a dermatologist.

My friend Liz went to a dermatologist in tenth grade for her acne and he put her on birth control. It was a win-win for Liz because it got rid of her acne, made her periods way better AND she didn't have to explain to her parents why she was on birth control. She actually started having sex since she was already on birth control anyway. I bet if my mom and dad had known that about Liz, they wouldn't have sent me to see a dermatologist.

I had a major crush on my dermatologist, Dr. Baker. He was super young and pretty hot. He looked too young to even be a doctor.

Dr. Baker suggested I do some special medicinal facial mask, like, every night. So I did that and the spot on my forehead kind of calmed down for a while. It faded to a pale rose color. But the spots on my thigh and foot didn't really change, so I just tried to forget about them. I tried to think of them as birthmarks, and I hoped that by the end of summer my tan would be dark enough that they would fade and eventually disappear. The sun usually makes my skin look better. When I wasn't at work, I made sure to always keep the spots on my foot and thigh covered up, which wasn't too hard, except no more booty-shorts or super short skirts, which was a drag. I covered the spot on my forehead with makeup and then wore my bangs over it and sometimes headbands and hats. If you look at any pictures of me from that time, I'll always have something pulled down over my forehead, so no one really knew. No one saw it. My parents knew. And my brother, Dean, who started calling me Scabby Abby. You wouldn't think that anyone could be such a colossal douche to their own sibling. Well, you've never met Dean.

So that went on for a while, but then the spot on my head started to get brighter and redder, so I stopped using the mask that Dr. Baker had prescribed because I was afraid that it was making it worse. I tried different masks and pastes and all sorts of crap. I tried oatmeal masks, avocado masks, egg whites and mud. I used toner, concealer, cover-up and finishing powder. I bought something called ScarFade from the drugstore. I "borrowed" Dad's credit card and bought a super-expensive skin-lightener off the

Internet that claimed to completely obliterate redness. Nothing worked. Plus, I was starting to look like the Marshmallow Man in the mornings, and sometimes my eyes would be so swollen that I could barely see. Also, I was grounded for a week for using Dad's credit card without permission and had to pay him back in monthly installments. I went back to see Dr. Jamieson. He thought maybe I was having an allergic reaction to something in my environment and sent me for an allergy test.

Allergy tests are really fun! Said no one ever. Except maybe some super-freak who wished he were a pincushion instead of a human. They poke up the insides of your arms with about a thousand different needles and then leave them in you for an hour while your skin swells up in some places but not in others. I found out I'm allergic to hay and rabbits. This meant pretty much buck-all to me since we don't live on a farm, I'm never around hay and I've always thought that rabbits were kind of stupid. I avoided anything remotely hay-ish or rabbity from that day forward, not that it was hard. The spots didn't go away.

That summer, my feet were cold all the time. They got so cold, they were numb. Every night, I wore my dad's big wool socks that he got in Alaska to bed. My feet went glacial at night. One night, I was dancing at a house party. I was in my bare feet on the dance floor because my high heels were slowing me down and I'd taken them off. Someone had dropped a beer bottle and it smashed all over the floor but everybody just kept dancing. Everybody else had shoes on. Not me. After about three or four more songs, my friend Marla pointed at my feet and said, "Dude, you're bleeding."

My feet were a mess, spiked with shards of glass and torn and bleeding all over the place. But the freakiest thing was, I didn't feel *anything*.

I went to the bathroom to wash my feet and get the glass out of them. The door to the bathroom was locked. I banged on the door. Nothing. I banged again, harder. I heard a low moan from behind the door. I turned around; a line had formed. Dustin Lorimer was behind me. He pointed to my feet. "You alright?"

I've had a massive crush on Dustin Lorimer since I was, like, five. His mom used to look after me and Dean when we were little. He lives the next street over.

I told Dustin that I was fine but I needed to get into the bathroom right away. He looked at my bloody feet again then stepped in front of me, threw his body against the bathroom door (HOT!) and the door popped open. Aaron Forsythe was in the empty bathtub looking like a sorry mess. He was drunk as fuck. It looked like he'd been crying and snot was running down his face.

I used to have a crush on Aaron Forsythe, but after seeing him like that, I didn't anymore. Obviously.

Aaron held his arm out with his fingers in the shape of a gun and pointed it at us.

"Get out of the tub, man. Abby needs to wash her feet," Dustin said.

"Why does she need to wash her feet?" Aaron slurred.

"I stepped in some glass," I said.

"Oh, *shiiit*," Aaron said, looking at my feet. He looked like he might projectile vomit on us. Dustin helped him stand up and climb out of the tub.

"What were you doing in the tub, Aaron?" Dustin said. "Or do I want to know?"

"Just thinking about stuff, you know. Sometimes you gotta think about stuff," Aaron said. "The bathtub is a really good place to think. Empty *or* full."

"I'll keep that in mind," Dustin said.

Aaron belched and staggered out of the bathroom clutching his studded belt. Dustin turned to me. I sat down on the edge of the tub and put my feet in. The glass in my feet scraped across the porcelain, the sound making us both wince.

"Are you sure you're alright?" Dustin said. "That looks pretty nasty."

"I think it'll be okay," I said, and turned on the tap. I wasn't sure if I should use hot or cold, but it turned out not to matter because wherever I turned the dial, it all felt like the same temperature.

"I'll get you a towel," Dustin said. He opened the tall cupboard across from the sink. I picked shards of glass out of my heel and toe. I wondered how the hell I wasn't feeling it, but I figured I'd had enough to drink that I didn't. I just didn't. That can happen with rye-gingers. Vodka-sodas too. Anything, really, if you drink enough of it. You just don't feel stuff. Not until the next day. But the next day came, and the day after that, and I had less and less feeling in my feet and I was getting another patchy weird spot behind my knee.

But that night at the party, I danced until dawn, I talked to boys, I flirted like mad—I looked smoking hot and I knew it. My feet bled, but I didn't care. It didn't matter. I wrapped them in maxi-pads and went home with my best friends, Marla and Liz. We cabbed back to Marla's house, and the three of us slept on her bed like a pile of puppies, our hair entwined, our arms and legs draped over each other. And I thought that it would always be that way. I thought my life would stay like that.

Summer started winding to a close, as it eventually does, and cheerleading tryouts had started at the end of August. This was twelfth grade, and I was pretty sure I would make the team again since I'd been on it the year before, but tryouts were still nerve-wracking. I had made the first cut, but there was still another round to get through, and then my interview.

One day, I got home from work and flopped down on the couch beside Dean. He was playing some stupid war video game. I looked at my hands. I had bitten all of my nails down to the quick, which I hate doing because they look so gross. I tugged off my socks then looked at Dean. He wasn't paying attention to me. He was shooting everything that moved. I bent my leg up and started to bite my big toenail. It's a shameful habit that I've had for as long as I can remember.

"Ugh, sick, Abby! How can you do that?" Dean kicked at my foot so I had to stop.

"I can't help it," I said. "I chewed off all of my fingernails. I have nothing else to bite."

"What are you? A vampire? You need to bite things all the time?"

"I'm anxious, okay?" I gingerly bit off the nail of my pinky toe and spat it at Dean. He shielded himself as if I'd thrown a knife at him.

"What the hell do *you* have to be anxious about? What? Was some little kid mean to you at the pool?"

"No."

"Three guys asked you out and you don't know which one to pick?"

"No."

"You're pregnant!" He pointed at me. "You got knocked up!" He laughed with glee. "I'm gonna be an uncle! Wait till I tell Mom and Dad! Or, should I say Grandma and Grandpa?"

"I'm not pregnant, you moron."

He shrugged. "What, then?"

"Cheerleading squad."

"Oh, *fuck* the cheerleading squad."

"You would," I said.

He thought about it for a moment. "Yeah, I would. Most of them. No, wait. All of them. Not you, though. That would be too weird. Even for me." He hit my foot away from my mouth again. "Stop that! You're going to make me puke! I'll puke on you! Is that what you want, Abby? Because I'll do it. *Blaaaah! Blaah!*" He pretended to barf all over me and I shoved him away. He shoved me back.

"Stop it."

"You stop it."

"You stop it first."

"I can only stop it if you stop it."

"Okay. Fine. I stopped, okay? I'm stopped. Happy?" I put my socks back on.

"Yep."

He went back to playing his video game. I bit the skin

around my cuticles and thought about all of the cheerleading stunts and combos I still couldn't do. And the ones that I *could* do, but couldn't land every single time. *Standing back handspring, step out, round-off, front handspring, step out, switch leap, front flip, front flip, full twisting layout.* I was going over the combo in my head that I wanted to do for the final tryout. I kept switching it around and around, adding and subtracting different stunts. Plus, I had to make up a cheer for this round of tryouts because they wanted us to be able to contribute to the cheer repertoire as well. I closed my eyes and started to mumble cheers I was inventing. After a few minutes, Dean turned to me and said, "Are you *sure* you're not pregnant?"

Like most ill-informed citizens, you might think that cheerleaders are all style and no substance. The lights are on but nobody's shopping. But you couldn't be more wrong. They say that the sign of first-rate intelligence is the ability to hold two opposing ideas in your mind at the same time and still retain the ability to function. Well, cheerleaders have to hold about seventy-eight opposing ideas in their minds at the same time and retain the ability to do backflips. You need to know to *the exact millisecond* when to twist, when to spin, when to stay still, when to arch, when to tuck, when to tumble, when to toss, when to jump, when to leap, when to fall and when to fly. *And* do all of it while maintaining perfect balance, often while *holding other people*, sounding off so loud that a whole stadium can hear you, smiling, always anticipating the next move while paying attention to the counts *and* keeping time with everyone else. Also, you have to be quick, smooth and precise while you do all of this *with enthusiasm*.

Stupid people can't be cheerleaders. They just can't. It's too complex. If you're stupid, you'll never make a great cheerleader. You should just play rugby instead.

A little while later, Mom came through the front door, carrying a bag of groceries.

"MOM! Abby's pregnant!" Dean yelled.

The bag of groceries dropped from my mom's arms and the eggs cracked their yellow mess all over the front hall. She stared at me.

"I'm not, Mom. I swear." I punched Dean in the shoulder, hard. "I'm not!"

"Are you sure?" Mom said, her voice shaky.

"Yeah." Dean turned to me. "How can you be sure, Abby?"

"You are such an ass," I said, scowling at him.

He grinned. "But seriously. How do you know for sure that you're not, Abby?"

"Because," I said.

"Because, why?"

"Because I'm a virgin, okay!" I threw my hands in the air. "There! *I'm a virgin!* Are you happy now?"

"Ha! I knew it!" Dean said, smug. He had been trying to get that out of me since the summer before. And I was super pissed at him in that moment for tricking me into having to admit it.

"But wait, Abby! What about immaculate conception? You could still be pregnant! Mom, you'd better get her a pregnancy test!"

"You're an idiot. I hate you!" I pounded his shoulder with my fist, but he only laughed at me and kept playing his video game. He was a pretty big guy and I couldn't really hurt him. Which was incredibly annoying. Especially when he pinned me down and farted on my head. There was nothing I could do then but wait it out.

"Dean. Clean up this mess," Mom said, and walked out of the room, her heels clacking over the tile.

"Ha!" I said, pointing at him. Then I went up to my room to practice my cheerleading moves in front of the mirror.

I had been working out all summer, trying to build my strength and endurance so I could make the cheer team, but I knew the competition was really tight. Plus, I'd been feeling a bit weak (which made sense, given what I know now), and I was nervous I wouldn't be able to land some of the stunts. Fifty-four girls had made the first cut, twenty-five would make the next cut, and fifteen or fewer would be on the team after those twenty-five had their interviews. Most of the cheerleaders on the squad last year were gymnasts or dancers, so they already had a lot of practice and training in those kinds of skills. I had never done either of those, but somehow made it onto the team in my junior year. I went through my closet and picked out what I was going to wear for the next tryout. A pleated yellow skirt (yellow is the most cheerful color!) and a red tank top (wearing red means you have confidence!). But red and yellow together? Ketchup and mustard. McDonald's. Ack! I hated all my clothes. I wanted to give them all away and start fresh with a whole new wardrobe. I called Marla. She picked up on the first ring.

"What are you wearing for the cheer tryout?"

"I don't know," she said. "Why? What are you wearing?"

"*I don't know.* That's why I'm calling *you!*"

"Are you alright?"

"No! I'm freaking out! I just tried on my cheer shoes from last year and they don't fit anymore! Ahhhhh!"

"Abby. Calm down. I'll come get you and we can go to the mall and buy you a new pair."

"Come over right now?"

"I'm on my way."

"You're the best."

"I know," she said.

I ran downstairs to ask Dad for the money for a new pair

of cheer shoes. He was at the kitchen counter, pummeling a lump of dough. He sighed when I asked him, wiped his hands on his jeans and fished two twenties out of his wallet and handed them to me. I kept holding out my hand.

"What?" he said.

"That's only forty dollars. Cheer shoes are, like, eighty dollars."

"Well, you get an allowance, don't you?"

"Yeah, but . . ."

"Sorry, Ab. That's all I have for you." He washed his hands at the sink. "You're going to have to cover the rest yourself."

"Fine." I stomped back upstairs and got my secret stash of cash out from under my mattress. It was only for emergencies or things I *really, really* needed. Cheer shoes were one of those things.

Marla honked the horn twice and I raced outside to meet her. I climbed into her little red Mini Cooper.

"Hi," I said.

"Seriously?" She reversed out of my driveway.

"What?"

"You're worried you're not going to make the team?"

"I don't know."

"You're going to make it, Abby. You're thin, you're gorgeous and you've got legs up to your freakin' eyeballs. You've got nothing to worry about. It's me who should be worried. I'm a fat cow."

"No you're not."

"I've gained eighteen pounds since last year," she said.

"Maybe it's muscle. Muscle weighs more than fat."

"Abby." She pinched some flesh on her stomach. "*This* is not muscle."

"Well, you're not fat."

"I'm a blimp."

"You're not going to go all anorexic again on me, are you?"

"If I have to."

"Marla, cheerleading is not about being skinny, okay? It's about having muscle and strength. If you're too skinny, you'll get weak and pass out. You *know* that."

She shrugged, sulking.

"Look, maybe you'll be a base."

"Yeah, *if* I even make the squad."

"Just remember, fifty percent of cheer is attitude . . . Kind of like life," I said, sticking my tongue in the corner of my cheek.

Marla rolled her eyes. "Oh, I'm definitely screwed then."

"Okay, shut up already. Help me decide what to wear."

"Alright, but first you have to tell me something. And I want the truth."

"What?"

"Why do you want to be a cheerleader so badly? You don't even like sports."

"I like cheer."

"Come on, Abby. You're taking this way too seriously. Why is this so important to you all of a sudden? Last year you didn't even care if you made the team or not. Liz and I *made* you try out."

I sighed. "Okay. *If* by some miracle I make the team this year and am really . . . *spirited* . . . I could be eligible for a full scholarship to USC."

Marla looked over at me. Gave me a slow blink.

"University of Southern California."

"I know what it stands for, Abby." She stared up at the stoplight in front of us, her jaw tight. When it turned to green, she pressed the gas too hard, making us lurch forward.

"It's one of the best acting schools in the country," I said, adjusting my seatbelt. "Probably *the* best. I'd never be able to afford the tuition though."

"What about the University of Texas?"

"I don't want to stay in Texas," I said.

"So you're just going to leave everyone behind? Your family? Your *friends*?"

"I've always wanted to be an actress, Marla. You know that."

"You've always been a drama queen, that's for sure." She pulled into a parking spot.

"Ex*cuse* me?"

"Nothing. Let's go get your shoes."

The morning of the tryout, I was so nervous I couldn't eat breakfast. I ended up wearing our team colors: my yellow skirt and a black tank top. I pulled my hair into a high ponytail and put a nice black bow in it. I looked at myself in the mirror. "You can do this," I said. Then I bounced around with my pom-poms for a little bit, psyching myself up. "S-P-I-R-I-T; who's got it? Me! Me! ME!"

There were three judges: Coach Clayton; the assistant coach, Miss Gable; and Rihanna Pilansky, head cheerleader. They all sat behind a long table and stared at me without smiling. I was so nervous my palms were wet. I rubbed them off on the soles of my shoes so they wouldn't be too slippery for when I did my stunts and tumbling.

"Hello, Abby," Coach Clayton said.

"Hi," I said.

"Are you ready?"

"Yes I am," I said, smiling.

They turned the music on and I did the routine I had practiced a hundred thousand times. *Keep smiling. Keep smiling no matter what. Don't you dare stop smiling.* I screwed up a little bit on landing my round-off but I just smiled bigger, hoping they'd overlook it. It was all kind of a blur. When I was finished, I didn't even know if I had done a good job or not. I didn't fall on my ass; that was the important thing.

The gym looked kind of wavy when I was done and I felt like I might pass out. I looked at the judges. They were all writing things down on their score sheets.

"Thank you, Abby," Coach Clayton said.

"Thank you for the opportunity," I said.

She nodded at me and smiled.

I gave them a wave and walked out of the gym, holding my head high and my shoulders back, my heart thudding in my ears.

Here's the thing about armadillos: they are the only creature on Earth other than humans that can get leprosy. If you've ever been to Texas, you know that we have a ditch-load of the giant pill-bugs running around, most of them, from what I've seen, end up as roadkill. Well, it turns out that around 20 percent of those armadillos are carrying the leprosy bacteria: *Mycobacterium leprae*. Who knows how *they* got it. I'm not even sure I *want* to know. Scientists think that new cases of leprosy in the United States could be from contact with infected armadillos. Like I said, *f'd-up*.

I don't really remember ever touching an armadillo, like, petting one or whatever. But maybe I did and just forgot. It's possible. I do remember when I was eleven and Dean was twelve, my parents put us in this Young Life church group—even though they aren't religious and never go to church—because they thought we could use some *structure* in our lives. Basically, we were fighting so much, they didn't know what to do with us. And, it was free. So we had to hang out with these other kids and the leaders, like, once a week for a year or something, and it sucked balls and we both hated it. Some of the guys were kind of cute, but they were too busy studying the Bible to notice me. Lame.

Anyway, I vaguely remember this one barbecue cookout thing they had, and I had a plate heaped with steak and hominy and coleslaw and potato salad and corn bread and all kinds of good stuff. I remember trying some meat that was kind of strong tasting, and squishy, like a sponge. I asked the leader what it was and he said armadillo meat. So, it's possible that I contracted leprosy that day. At a *church* barbecue. Which pretty much means that if there is a God, He *wanted* me to get leprosy. He practically *gave* it to me Himself. Thanks, God. What a great gift. You shouldn't have, really.

Why didn't the rest of the people at the barbecue get leprosy then, you're probably asking (I know you're asking that because that's what I asked). Well, because all of the other people there who ate that armadillo were in the 95 percent of the population naturally immune to the bacteria that causes leprosy. Nothing happens to them. They don't get nerve damage, they don't get sores, they don't get fevers, weakness, numb feet and all the other crap, *nothing*.

And *me*, lucky, lucky me, I'm in the 5 percent of the population that is *not* immune to the bacteria.

I know what you're thinking; I should sue the youth group. I should sue the church. I should sue GOD HIMSELF!!!! I should. And I would if I could. But how could I prove it? There's no way to prove it. It was *six years ago*. Also, suing the church won't make my face and hands and feet look the way they used to. They won't bring back what were supposed to be some of the "best years of my life." It wouldn't undo any of it. They always say that life isn't fair, well, I'm living proof of that. There is no fair in life, it just is.

I ended up making the cheerleading squad, and, needless to say, was thrilled. The other thing about being a cheerleader is that guys pay attention to cheerleaders. Suddenly, it's like you go from pretty-hot to super-hot. If you're actually ugly, or a butter-face, and you are on a cheerleading squad, guys can't tell that you're ugly. Based solely on the fact that you're a cheerleader, it's a given that you're also hot. It's like a shield. A cloaking device. That's what cheerleading can do for a person. But you have to earn it. You have to be light and limber and eat healthy pretty much all the time so you don't gain too much weight or else you'll be too heavy to toss around or stand on people's shoulders. You have to practice all the time, like, every day, and stretch and stretch and stretch so you're flexible enough to do the splits or put your leg behind your head or arch backward while balancing in someone's hands. But you also have to be strong enough, so you have to do push-ups and sit-ups and calisthenics too. Then you'll wake yourself up at night chanting *5, 6, 7, 8!* in your sleep.

Cheerleading's a buck-load of work. But if I got a full scholarship, it would all be worth it.

I made the final cut of the cheerleading squad just before school started. In the second week of school, Jude Mailer asked me out. I said yes. Obviously.

Jude Mailer was one of the hottest guys in school. Ask anyone. Like me, he was in twelfth grade. He played forward on the boys' basketball team. He was tall, but not gangly awkward tall, just nice, let me reach that for you, tall. He did sometimes bump his head in doorways, but I thought that was kind of cute.

The day he did it was a Monday, so I figure he must've been thinking about it all weekend. I sat with Marla and Liz in the cafeteria. I was picking at Liz's fries even though I wasn't supposed to eat junk like that because I had to keep my weight down if I wanted to be a flyer on the squad, which I did. The flyer is the person who gets vaulted to the top of a pyramid to perform a stunt. They are the lightest, most agile, most balanced people on the team. Flyers didn't eat French fries. But all three of us had made the squad that year, so we felt justified.

"Who do you think will be a flyer this year?" Marla asked.

"Carrie Nelson, probably," Liz said. "She's so . . ."

"Compact?" I said.

"Bitchy. I was going to say bitchy," Liz said.

"I wouldn't call her a bitch per se," Marla said. "She's just a flighty little tart."

"You hardly even know her," I said.

"I know," said Liz. "But doesn't she just come across as . . ."

"Bitchy?" Marla said.

"Yeah!" said Liz.

"Have you ever really talked to her though?" I asked.

"Not really," Liz said. "But I can just tell these things. I have bitch-dar. It's like gaydar but for bitches."

"Maybe you were picking up your own signal," I said.

Marla started cracking up and Liz got fake-mad and threw a fry at me. I caught it and ate it. Then Jude came up to our table. Everyone went quiet for a minute. Then Liz giggled.

"Hey," he said, looking at me, then, briefly, at Marla and Liz.

"Hey," I said.

Marla gave him a little wave and Liz moved over, gesturing that he should sit down. He sat beside her, directly across from me. "How's it going, Abby?"

"Good . . . Great," I said.

Marla and Liz, after staring at him for a bit and making everything awkward, finally got the hint and made up an excuse to leave the table. Marla gave me the double thumbs-up as they walked away and Liz fanned herself with both hands.

"Would you want to go out with me this weekend?" he said.

Don't panic. Don't panic. Don't panic. You're a cheerleader. You're hot. He's a basketball player. He's hot. You belong together. It's only natural. "Sure," I said. *Maybe that wasn't enthusiastic enough. He thinks you're not into him. He thinks you hate him!* "Yeah, definitely."

"Cool," he said, grinning. "Let me get your number." He took out his phone and punched my number into it. As far as I know, it's still in there.

Jude and I had a lot in common. He liked going to the movies; I liked going to the movies. He liked black licorice; I liked black licorice. That's enough to base a relationship on, right? He was pretty quiet, actually. We didn't talk much. But sometimes, just being quiet with someone is as nice as talking, or sometimes better. He never called me. Not once. He would text me back after I texted him, usually. But he never called. At first I was pissed off about that, but eventually, I didn't care anymore. He was a hot basketball player, he had his own car and he was my boyfriend. Because I was on the cheerleading squad, I was at all of his home games, and all of his away games too. I probably would have gone to them even if I hadn't been cheering them though, because that's what good girlfriends do. I was a good girlfriend, I think. I never told him what to do or what to wear or that he shouldn't hang out with his friends, which I know a lot of other girls do. I bought him little presents, like sweatbands and cinnamon hearts. Do you know how hard it is to find cinnamon hearts when it's not February? Nine out of ten on the difficulty meter, with ten being impossible. I even stayed after school sometimes to watch Jude's basketball practices while I did my homework. Even though I don't really like basketball, I liked watching Jude play.

The only thing I can say to describe him on the court was that it was like watching poetry in motion. He was a graceful gazelle. He made basketball look like a dance. I could tell he was more agile than I was, even before the leprosy bug was doing nasty and horrible things inside my body.

Jude liked to get a hamburger and a milkshake from Mitzy's Diner after his practices. I'd usually go with him and get fries with gravy.

"Fries with gravy *and* ketchup is disgusting," Jude said, staring at my plate.

"But fries with ketchup are good," I said.

"Agreed."

"And fries with gravy are good."

"Uh-huh."

"So why can't fries with ketchup and gravy be good?"

"One or the other, Abby. Not both."

I looked down at my plate. The brown and red swirled together over the mess of fries. It did look kind of gross. I shrugged, ate a fry. "If you say so," I said.

Jude sighed.

"Are you this particular about all your food or just French fries?"

"I care about food," he said. "I *respect* food."

"Uh-huh."

"This." He gestured to my plate. "This is not respect."

I ate another fry, grinning at him. "But it sure is tasty."

He gazed over my shoulder toward the kitchen. "I think I might like to be a chef," he said.

"Ooh la la."

"It wouldn't have to be a fancy place, like, fine dining or anything. Just simple, good food done right."

"Maybe you could have your own food truck," I said.

"No. I would be way too cramped in one of those. Plus, I'm not even done growing. I'm probably going to get even taller than this."

I nodded, chewing another fry.

"I was thinking more like my own restaurant."

"Oh yeah? That would be cool. What would it be called?"

"Jude's," he said, like it should have been obvious. Then he smiled dreamily like he could see it all materializing just as he imagined. The server came then and cleared our plates. She gave me a wink. I watched Jude stare after her as she walked away. I coughed into my hand.

"What about basketball?" I said.

"What about it?"

"You're so good."

He wiped his mouth on his napkin and scrunched it into a ball. "Not that good." He launched it into my nearly empty water glass. It landed at the bottom, soaking up the ice water.

"You're—"

"Not good enough to play pro ball. It's a high school team, Abby. It's not a career." He took a big drink from his milkshake and set down his cup. I guess someone somewhere had told him he wasn't good enough. And maybe they were right. I didn't know. "What about you?" he said.

"What *about* me?"

"What do you want to do?"

"I . . . I want to be an actress," I said.

He screwed up his face a little, assessing me.

I picked at my nail polish. "I want to be famous," I mumbled into the table.

"What?"

"I WANT TO BE FAMOUS!"

Some old people turned around to look at us. A little kid in a nearby booth laughed and screeched. Our server looked up from her cash register.

"Why?" Jude said.

"I don't know," I said. "It's just something I've always wanted. I've always known. I want to get out of Texas and I want to be famous."

"You couldn't be famous in Texas?"

I shook my head. "I don't belong here," I said.

"What? You're too good for Texas?"

"No, no. It's not that. It's just a feeling. Like, I don't know how to describe it . . ."

"Relax. I'm just kidding."

"Oh."

Jude studied me. I could feel his eyes running up and down my body. Over my breasts, my collarbones, my cheeks, my hair. "Yep, I could see that working out for you."

I exhaled. I hadn't realized I'd been holding my breath.

"You're a total babe," he said and took out a pack of gum, offering me a piece before popping one in his mouth.

"Thanks," I laughed, and wondered if I was blushing.

"Hollywood?" he said.

"Yeah. Well, hopefully."

"How are you going to get there?"

"Cheerleading."

He raised his eyebrows.

"I'm playing the long game."

By this time, I had lost almost all of the feeling in both of my feet, which made climbing to the top of a pyramid, or balancing on people's hands, *extremely* difficult. My hands and wrists were starting to bother me. They'd get, like, a buzzing feeling, which was different from pain but definitely didn't feel right. I thought I'd been texting too much and maybe had carpal tunnel syndrome or something. I knew that could happen, that it was pretty common, so I didn't worry too much about it. My feet I attributed to poor circulation, inherited from my mother's side. I started to get fevers and night sweats. I thought I had a weird flu that wouldn't go away. Sometimes I got headaches, but everyone gets headaches. Don't they? When I knew I had a fever, I'd just take a couple of Tylenol and have a cold bath and get into bed with a cold washcloth on my head. It was usually gone by the morning. I also got tired a lot. Usually when I got home from school or cheer practice, I felt weak. I thought I was just hungry, so I'd have a huge snack, then go chill out for a while on the couch or in my room. One time, I fell asleep after school and slept right through dinner and through the whole night.

The next morning when I walked into the kitchen, my mom handed me a cup of coffee. "I couldn't wake you up last night," she said. "I thought you were dead in there."

"Her breath sure smells like she died," Dean said.

"Shut up, Dean," I said.

"Monkey-butt is how I would describe it. With a little side of skunk."

"Are you feeling alright?" Mom felt my forehead.

"Yeah," I said.

"Abby. It's called halitosis, okay?" Dean said. "There are things you can do to manage your problem. It doesn't have to ruin your life."

"Would you *please* shut up?"

"Floss. Mouthwash. Toothpaste. Have you heard of toothpaste?"

I turned my back on Dean and looked out the window. Mrs. Greely was out watering her garden. She was about ninety years old but still did all her own yard work. She called me Tabby, but I let her. It seemed right for her to call me that. Maybe you're a different person to everyone you know.

"I want us to go back to the doctor this week," Mom said. "I'll make you an appointment today."

"Dr. Jamieson doesn't know anything," I said. "Besides, I have cheer practice every afternoon this week, a quiz on

Thursday and a test on Friday. I don't have *time* to go to the doctor."

"I can take you to a different doctor if you want, but you're going to have to miss practice one day this week so we can go."

"I was just *tired*, Mom. I'm *fine*. Teenagers need a lot of sleep! I'm normal, okay? Marla sleeps, like, fourteen hours a day."

"She's on her back fourteen hours a day, I'd believe that," Dean said. He made the face where you put your tongue in your cheek and move your fist so it looks like you're giving a blow job. I wanted to hit him in the mouth, but I didn't.

"I'm fine, Mom. I'm not sick."

She pressed her lips together. "Do it as a personal favor to me, then," she said.

"Can I do it as a personal favor to you next week? When I don't have, like, fifty million things to study for?"

She sighed. "Alright," she said. "I'll make your appointment today."

"You might ask if they can do something for your breath, too, while you're there," Dean said, fanning his hand in front of his face.

I leaned toward him and blew my morning breath all over him.

That day I ate lunch with Marla and Liz. Jude and his friend Brett joined us at our table. Jude slid his tray in beside mine and gave me a little kiss on the cheek.

"How's it going?" he said.

"Urrgh," I said, gesturing to my pile of textbooks.

"That good, hey?"

It was the lead-up to Christmas break and the teachers had it out for us. We had hundreds of assignments and they gave pop quizzes almost every day. I needed to keep my grades high so I could get into USC and stay on the cheer-leading squad through the rest of the year. Marla, Liz and I burned off steam at lunch like we usually did, by making fun of other people.

Clint Rasmussen walked by us, mouth breathing, checking his phone. "What must it be like to go through life with a head shaped like a potato?" Marla said, her eyes following Clint.

"You know where he's from, don't you?" I said.

"Not a clue."

"Idaho."

"No."

"That would explain a few things," Liz said.

"He's actually really lucky," I said. "When he wants hash browns, all he needs to do is shave his face."

Liz made a disgusted face, sticking her tongue out the side of her mouth.

Dale Romanchuk was coming our way. He was a

mangled-looking kid who could never quite keep it together. Greasy hair. Glasses. A face full of acne. His clothes were always wrinkled and mis-buttoned. Liz pushed her backpack out a little. Dale tripped over it, spilling his drink, nearly falling, but catching himself at the last minute.

We laughed, covering our mouths.

"That wasn't very nice," Jude said.

"Yeah, Liz," I said. "It's not his fault his parents are cousins."

She and Marla laughed.

"Boom. Boom. Boom," Liz said as Heather O'Leary walked by our table.

"That's gotta be at least a five point two on the Richter scale," I said.

Heather glanced over her shoulder at us. Liz made a mean face back at her, and we giggled as she turned away again, smoothing her hair.

"I think she's actually lost weight since last year," Marla said.

"No. She just started wearing baggier clothes," I said. "It's an optical illusion."

"Huh," she said. "Maybe I should try that."

Uber-geek Brian Tate stood in the pizza lineup, just out of earshot. I gestured toward him with my chin. "Excuse me," I said, emulating his squeaky voice, "but do you know what the square root of I will never get laid is?" Liz and Marla cracked up. Bailey Lovell and Caleb Markowski walked by our table. He was super short and she was really tall. "Here come Brontosaurus and T-rex," Marla said.

"Mwaarr!" I dug my elbows into my sides, making little T-rex arms. Liz bobbed her head, stretching her neck up and down, impersonating a brontosaurus. She and I pretended to try to kiss each other and not be able to reach the other's lips, all the while making dinosaur sounds. We laughed. We laughed so hard we collapsed into each other, unable to breathe.

"She's actually a really good basketball player," Jude said.

"At least she's good at something," I said. "I've seen her biology quizzes. She's failing everything."

"We took art together last year," Liz said. "All she made all year were these circles that looked like nipples. A dot in the middle and a circle surrounding it. Charcoal? Boobs. Pastel? Boobs. Watercolor? Boobs. Clay? Boobs. She's, like, obsessed with boobs or something. We called it boob-art. Bailey's boob-art."

We laughed.

"I like boobs," Brett said.

"Isn't that wonderful for you?" Marla said.

He grinned at her.

"We gotta go," Jude said, standing. He cocked his head at Brett and Brett stood up too. I leaned my cheek toward Jude for a kiss, but none came. "See you later," he said. Then they were gone.

By the time my doctor's appointment came, I had another scaly red spot on my chest, right above my left boob. Mom took me to a new doctor named Dr. Lee. She was short with dark hair and dark eyes that looked like they'd seen a lot of sad stuff. I sat on the little bed-thing and showed her the spots and told her everything. She looked closely at each of the spots and touched them all. Then she turned to the sink and washed her hands.

"Are you sexually active, Abby?" Dr. Lee asked.

"Um, how do you define . . . active?" I said.

She smiled.

Jude and I had fooled around a bit. I wasn't saving myself for marriage or anything, I just, I don't know. I wanted to be in love. Is that stupid? It's stupid. I know. But you only get one first time! Just one! I wanted to be sure. Jude was super-sweet and really nice to me and a great kisser. I thought that maybe he could be the one I would lose my virginity with, but I still wasn't 100 percent sure. I felt like I was still getting to know him.

"I've never had sex," I said, hanging my head.

"That's nothing to be ashamed of, Abby. It's perfectly normal."

"Okay," I said. "It's just that all of my friends have. So it doesn't exactly feel normal."

"There's absolutely no harm in waiting. In fact, I highly recommend it," she said.

I nodded.

"You play sports?"

"I'm a cheerleader."

"Really? That's great."

"Thanks."

"Would you say that you sweat a lot?"

"I would say that I sweat a normal amount," I said. I sniffed at my armpit. "Why? Do I smell? Do I have body odor?" I was horrified.

"No, no. Nothing like that," Dr. Lee said. Then she pulled out her phone and started swiping away. I hate when doctors do that. Are they texting? Are they looking something up on WebMD? Nobody knows.

"I'm fairly confident that the spots on your skin are tinea versicolor. I'm going to give you a fungicide that should clear them up. As for the muscle weakness and fatigue, I'd like you to take an iron supplement and make sure that you're eating properly, with plenty of protein in every meal, and not skipping meals. Also, you should be getting at least eight hours of sleep every night, preferably more, without exception."

"Sorry, fungus?"

"Yes. Tinea versicolor is a yeast that lives on the skin and causes irregular discolored patches. It's common for people your age who are physically active and often sweating or in the heat to experience it."

"Like, ringworm?"

"Yes."

"Because that's what Dr. Jamieson thought I had and he already gave me an antifungal cream and it didn't work."

"Probably wasn't a strong enough dosage," she said. "I'll give you a pill to take orally in addition to an antifungal cream." She pulled out her prescription pad and started scribbling. "Nothing to worry about. Although, I'll warn you, even though your spots will most likely disappear after you've been taking the pills for a week or so, they may come back if you're hot and sweating a lot, like in the summer." She tore the prescription off and handed it to me. "You'll be fine," she said.

S he was wrong.

M arla and Liz and I went shopping in ████████ a few weeks later. I rifled through a rack of striped sweaters. "I think I'm going to have sex with Jude," I announced. Liz squealed, clutching a cardigan to her chest.

"Finally," Marla said. "It's been, like, what?"

"Almost three months," I said.

"Christ, I'm surprised he's stuck around this long."

"Marla!" Liz said. "Be nice."

"What?" Marla said.

Liz shrugged. "We thought maybe you were saving your-self for marriage or something." The three of us looked at each other for a moment. Then we all cracked up.

"No, no, no, but are you *sure*, Abby? Are you, like, *really* sure?" Liz said. "Because you know," she lowered her voice, "toast can't ever be bread again."

"Yeah, I mean, it's like Marla said. At this point, we're either going to have sex or break up and . . . I don't want to break up."

"Have you talked about it?" Marla said.

I shook my head. "Jude doesn't really talk much."

Liz nodded. "The strong, silent type."

"Something like that," I said.

"Maybe he'll speak more through body language," Marla said, coming at me, grinding up against my leg.

"Stop!" I laughed, pushing her away.

"Okay, okay." Liz flapped her hands. "When are you going to do it?"

"*Where* are you going to do it?" Marla said.

"I was thinking the night of our three-month anniversary. We're going for dinner at Rydell's. I made reservations."

"Rydell's?"

I shrugged. "He likes food. It's a foodie place."

"Don't eat too much," Liz said. "You don't want to do it on a full stomach."

"So then . . . back to his place?" Marla said.

"I don't know."

"*Your* place?"

"I don't *know*."

"Not his car, Abby. Please, God, not his car. You're too good for that," Marla said.

"Probably not his car," I said.

She made a face.

"But maybe."

Liz squealed, laughing.

"The back seats fold down." I shrugged.

Marla shook her head.

"Do you need condoms?" Liz asked. She opened her purse and pulled out a gray strip of little plastic packets. "Here. These are the good kind. Not that cheap saran wrap the school nurse hands out." She slapped them into my hand.

"Thanks," I said. I shoved them away in my bag.

"Our little Abby," Marla said, putting her arm around my shoulder. "Growing up so fast."

I figured by the time our three months rolled around the pills and cream would have worked on my new blemishes. I didn't want Jude to see the angry red spots and was careful to hide them from him, from everyone. I hated looking at them, touching them, even knowing they were there, but I kept taking the pills and applying the new fungicide

41

every day, three times a day, believing they would eventually go away.

Jude and I never made it to our three-month anniversary. Jude dumped me two days before. Just out of the blue. No warning. Bam! In a *text*. After we had been dating for *three months*. Which is a long time, in high school. In high school, days are like light years. You have all the time in the world, and that world belongs to the young, and you *are* young; you will never die, and you will always be beautiful.

The worst part was that right after Jude dumped me, IN A TEXT, he started going out with Carrie Nelson. Like two days later. But, whatever. I'm over it. Obviously.

Marla and Liz were there to console me and bring me ice cream and tell me what an ass-hat they always thought Jude was and that I was better off without him, because that's what friends are for. They made a list of all the guys I could potentially go out with to get back at Jude.

"Okay, Abby," Marla said, "let's face it. You're one of the hottest girls in school. You could get any guy you want."

"But I don't want to go out with someone just to get back at Jude. I only want to go out with someone I actually like."

"Ugh, that's so mature of you," Liz said.

"Okay, who do you like, then?" Marla asked.

"I don't know."

"Come on!"

"Dustin Lorimer?" I said.

"Oh, *gawd*!" Liz said.

"What?"

"He's so . . . boy next door."

"Yeah, he lives one street over from me."

"Really? Dustin? He's so vanilla," Marla said.

"What's wrong with vanilla?" I said.

"It's boring!"

"I kind of like vanilla," I mumbled. "As a flavor."

They laughed at me. "Who else?" Marla said.

"I know who you could go out with to make Jude really mad," Liz said.

"Who? Who?" Marla said, getting her pen ready.

"Nate Russell."

Marla squealed and wrote his name on the list in her big, bubbly cursive.

"No way," I said.

"Oh, come on. He's sexy."

"He's about as sexy as a sasquatch," I said. "He smells like one too."

Nate Russell was a skater boy. He had long hair and a nose-ring, *between* his nostrils, like a bull. He and his friends had a huge hate-on for all jocks and preps, which, of course, included cheerleaders.

"Even if I *did* like him, which I don't, he would never go out with me," I said. "He hates people like us."

"He only hates us because he can't *be* us," Marla said.

"I don't think so," I said.

"Maybe *I* should ask him out," Liz said. "Do you think?"

"Sure. If you want to set yourself up for a harsh rejection, go for it," I said.

She pouted a little and then went over to my makeup table and started putting on my boysenberry lipstick. "Maybe I should reinvent myself," she said. "I could make myself into the kind of girl that Nate *would* go out with." She picked up a black eye-pencil and began to draw heavy outlines around her eyes with little wings at the edges. "I could probably learn to skateboard. How hard could it be?"

Marla and I looked over at her. She looked like a blonde raccoon. "Why would you want to do that?" I said.

"Well, I have really good balance already," she said. "Plus some of those tricks look pretty fun. You know, like, ollie. Kick-flip. I could totally do a kick-flip."

"No, I mean, why would you want to reinvent yourself

for a guy? Don't you want a guy who likes you the way you are? Who likes what you've already invented?"

She shrugged. "I'm only sixteen. I don't even know what I am yet."

Marla and I looked at each other.

"Maybe I'm actually a punk rocker hiding inside a cheer-leader." Liz kissed the mirror and made a big pink lip-print in the corner. I've never wiped it off.

We made popcorn and watched *Bring It On* and talked about cheerleading for a while. I told them I was afraid of falling.

"How embarrassing would it be to fall flat on your ass in front of an entire stadium?"

"You have to have faith in your squad, Abby," Marla said. "Someone will always be there to catch you."

"Yeah," Liz said. "We would never let you fall, Abby."

And, you know, people can say that, and you hope that they're right, and you want to believe them, but sometimes, there's just not anyone there to catch you when you fall. I know it's hella cheesy to say, but it's another way that cheerleading is like life. And when you hit the ground, does it hurt?

Yes, it most certainly does.

That weekend, Liz, Marla and I went to a house party. It was a big party, the last big one before the holidays. I drank way too much. Jude was there. He was wearing a black T-shirt, jeans and a hat. He looked really good. I avoided him for most of the night, although we had a few awkward moments where one of us caught the other one looking at the other then quickly looked away. Once I was good and buzzed, I sidled up to him on the couch. He was talking to Brett but I interrupted them.

"Hi, Jude," I said, then burped.

"Hey, Abby."

"I gotta get another beer," Brett said, standing. "You want one?" He pointed at Jude.

Jude nodded.

"Where's Carrie?" I said.

"She's sick," he said.

"Aw." I pouted. "I hope it's not an STI."

"That's not funny," he said.

"Oh, no, I didn't mean for it to be," I said. "I was serious."

He shook his head.

The booze had emboldened me. I went for it. "Jude, why did you break up with me?"

He stared straight ahead. The muscles of his jaw clenched.

"Was it because I didn't have sex with you?"

"No." He rubbed his thumb against his palm.

"Because I was going to. I wanted to."

"That had nothing to do with it," he said.

"Is it because I'm not pretty enough?"

He turned to me, his eyes scanned over my body, my face. He shook his head, adjusted his hat.

"Well, why did you then?"

He sighed. "You're hot as hell, Abby. But . . . you're not a very nice person."

My eyes stung. I felt acrid bile rising in my throat. "Oh," I said, like an idiot. My stomach felt hard and hollow as though I'd been hit. I got up off the couch, went upstairs to the bathroom and threw up.

I'm not proud of this, but I ended up having sex that night, in the laundry room, with Chad Bennett. I don't love Chad Bennett. I don't know if anybody does. Maybe his mother. Maybe. He's the biggest player in ▮▮▮▮▮▮ and has probably slept with half the town. I won't say he took advantage of me. I knew what I was doing. I think I wanted to get back at Jude. I don't know. It was sloppy, it hurt and somehow my new red halter top got bleach stains all over it. At one point, Chad ran his hand across a sore on my inner thigh, then recoiled as if he'd been bitten. I felt so ashamed. But that wasn't even the worst part. The worst part was, we didn't use a condom. For a smart girl, I can be a real moron sometimes. That was one of those times. I don't know why we didn't. My bag wasn't in the room. He didn't have one on him. It was so stupid. Afterwards, while he pulled his jeans on, buttoned his shirt, I blurted out, "Am I a nice person, Chad?"

He looked up at me, ran a hand over his face. "Yeah, baby. You're real nice. The nicest." He leaned in, kissed my lips. I closed my eyes. "I have to go," he whispered. "Sorry."

When I opened my eyes again, I was alone in the darkness of the laundry room, sitting on top of the dryer, the smell of bleach burning my nostrils.

Chad didn't ask for my number, and I was glad. I didn't care if I ever saw him again. Marla and Liz asked how it was as we stumbled back to Marla's house in the pale light of dawn.

"I don't think you really need to ask, do you?" I said. "You already know."

They laughed and groaned because it was true. Both of them had already slept with Chad. I felt dirty and stupid. I wished I could do the night over again. I wished I could have my virginity back.

When I'm old and gray and looking back on my life, my greatest regrets, I'm pretty sure that one will be near the top of the list.

I was kind of a mess over Christmas break, obsessing over what Jude had said. Was it true? *Was* I a mean bitch? Did everyone know it except me? I didn't think I was, but maybe I actually was. I thought about all of the times we made fun of people. We were just blowing off steam; we didn't really mean it. Everyone did that crap. I'd been called bitchy before, sure, but, somehow, it wasn't the same as what Jude had said. It didn't bother me as much. I didn't tell anyone what he had said. Not even Marla. I tried not to think about it and instead constantly checked myself for signs of an STI or symptoms of pregnancy. I'd send Marla and Liz desperate texts saying things like: WHY DID I DO THAT??? I'M SUCH AN IDIOT!!!

To which Marla would reply: At least you got it over with. Won't be so much pressure next time.

And Liz would text back things meant to make me laugh, like: Mom?

Eventually, I just had to accept the fact that I had lost my virginity to Chad Manwhore Bennett. There was no going back in time. There was no un-toasting the bread.

Not long after that, in early January, I took a really bad fall during a football game that we were cheering at ▮▮▮▮▮ High, an away game. I was climbing to the top of a pyramid to do a stunt; I was an alternate-flyer because

Carrie was away that day. Who knew where she was. Probably with Jude Mailer. Probably being super nice to every living thing. But anyway, I was the flyer that day. Long story short, I had a very poor execution of a front-tuck-somersault from the top of a pyramid of human bodies and ended up falling, twisted and mangled, from about eighteen feet in the air. It was no one's fault but my own. Nobody dropped me. It was the leprosy bug. Getting in my nerves, my muscles. I thought I could do it; I knew I should have been able to. I was nimble. I was lithe. I was agile as a cat. But that was the *old* me, before the leprosy got in and fucked up my shit. I know that now. Leprosy made me do it. I wonder how many things you could use that for?

Abby, your room is a pigsty!

Leprosy made me do it.

Abby, you killed your brother!

Leprosy made me do it.

Abby, you stole a truckload of diamonds!

Leprosy made me do it.

Maybe?

I broke my collarbone, my left hand (my dominant hand) and wrist, my right wrist, both ankles and my right foot. It seems weird that I would break so much, but I think that was the bug doing its work. The bones of my fingers and hands, toes and feet were already weakening. See, it literally eats you away, from the inside out. Liz said my head bounced off the ground when I hit it. I suffered a serious head injury and was in a coma for sixteen days.

Being in a coma is probably what being dead is like. It's like a dress rehearsal for death. I didn't have any dreams. I didn't ever know when anyone was in the room with me or talking to me or sticking tubes in my arm or up my nose. I didn't see anything. I didn't hear any voices or see any bright light beckoning me toward it. I was just gone.

While I was in that hospital bed, my body seriously started to deteriorate. It was like my immune system just rolled over and gave up and said, "Okay, leprosy, you can take over now. We're done here." I developed more lesions. All over my face and body. And they had papules. My body blistered and boiled. I don't want to describe it here in too much detail because you'll sick yourself, but let's just say I was disgusting.

Mom and the nurses kept putting the fungicide on me, three times a day, every day, but it wasn't working. Obviously.

The attending doctor at the hospital, Dr. Neal, prescribed a steroid cream that the nurses put on me and this actually strengthened the leprosy bacteria and made it go into hyperactive mode; *this is leprosy on steroids.* So the spots multiplied again and started turning bumpy and some of the spots on my face turned into giant lumps, the size of walnuts. My lips grew thick and rubbery. At one time, I had wished that I had fuller lips, but not like this. This was grotesque. This was a nightmare incarnate. I guess that's why they say be careful what you wish for . . .

When I came out of my coma, it was like waking up inside a terrible horror movie. And the monster was me.

My family sat in the hospital room, watching and waiting.

"Abby? Abby?" my mom said. "I think she's awake." She came and stood beside the bed and held my hand. I could see that she was holding my hand, but I couldn't feel it. "Greg, go get the doctor," she said. My dad hurried from the room.

"Mommy?" I said. My voice was scratchy and raw. It didn't even sound like my voice.

"Oh, Abby! I'm here, sweetie. I'm right here. Everything's going to be alright."

"What's wrong? What happened?"

"You're in the hospital, honey. You fell. Do you remember?"

I remembered everything, eventually. It came back slowly, over the next few hours. I felt a cold spike in my stomach when I remembered about Jude and Carrie, what Jude had said, and how I was only the flyer on the day that I fell because Carrie had been away. What if she had been there? Would I still be in the hospital? Broken and mangled? Who could ever know. And I felt an icy splintering in my guts when I remembered what I had done with Chad. I wondered if the whole school already knew. I wondered what he had said about me.

"You look like Pizza-the-Hut," Dean said, grinning down at me. "Maybe you could actually get an acting career now."

"Dean. Out. Now," Mom said.

I looked down at myself. Both my hands and wrists were in casts, as well as my right foot and both ankles. Then I noticed all the new spots on my arms.

"He's just glad to see you," Mom said, brushing a tear away.

My face felt all tight and puffy. My lips didn't feel right when I spoke. It was like that time the dentist had frozen my mouth and I couldn't talk or drink properly. "Mom," I said. "Show me a mirror."

"I don't think that's a good idea, Abby," she whispered.

"Mom—"

"You've just come out of a coma. You're probably in shock."

"WHAT'S WRONG WITH ME?"

"Shh, baby girl. It's okay. You're alright."

"What happened? You have to tell me, Mom. Do I have AIDS? Am I dying?"

My mom looked around the room, frantic. "Your dad's gone to get the doctor. They'll be back any minute. He'll explain everything."

I started to cry. When you wake up from a coma and you can't feel your fingers or feet, you have a broken collarbone, a broken hand, two broken wrists, a broken foot, and scabby, bulbous sores all over your body, you cry. It's just what you do.

Dr. Neal had run a series of blood tests and a urinalysis to see what the hell was wrong with me, but of course everything showed up negative because the way to test for leprosy is from a skin scraping, a biopsy, which they hadn't done. So, as usual, no one knew buck-all. Dr. Neal thought it was some kind of autoimmune response to the stress of the breakup, and then the bad fall, and that it would go away in time. They released me from the hospital after a few more days and I had to use a wheelchair to get around because of my broken ankles and foot. I slept on the couch downstairs since I couldn't get up to my room. I couldn't even get to the bathroom myself, because of my broken hand and wrists, I couldn't wheel myself in the chair. Talk about embarrassing.

I spent most of my time on the Internet, trying to self-diagnose. Dean set up a speech-recognition program on my laptop for me so I didn't have to use my hands to type.

For a while I was convinced that Chad Bennett had given me a nasty case of syphilis or a new STI that hadn't even been named yet. Either that, or I had HIV or full-blown AIDS. That would be just my luck, the very first time I have sex, I would get AIDS. I hated myself. I hated Chad Bennett. I hated everyone in Texas. And everyone in the world, besides.

I was the most hideous creature to ever exist. The Elephant Man had nothing on me. My life was over. And I was glad. I would rather die than look like a circus sideshow for the rest of my life. This wasn't supposed to happen. My senior prom was coming up in the spring and I was in the running to be prom queen! I cried under my blankets for most of the day, every day. I refused to leave the house or let anyone see my face. Even my family. Marla and Liz came over to bring me my homework and black licorice and magazines, but I told my parents I didn't want to see anyone, so they never got past the front door.

"Is she contagious?" I heard Marla ask.

"We don't know," my mom said quietly.

"What's wrong with her?" Liz said.

"We don't know."

"Okay . . ." Marla said. I could hear the doubt in her voice. "Well, tell her we love her," she said. "And . . . we miss her."

"I will, honey. Thanks."

I heard Mom close the door softly behind them. She came into the living room and set the magazines and candy and pile of homework on the coffee table then sat down beside me.

"Are you sure you don't want to see them, Abby? It might be good for you."

"No." I shook my head. "Absolutely not."

Mom sighed. "Okay." She reached out to touch my hair and I flinched, turned away from her. She put her hands in her lap. "It won't be like this forever."

"Yeah, but what if it is?"

"It won't be."

"Okay," I said. Then I covered my head with a blanket and curled up in a ball, letting tears slide over my face and soak into the couch cushions.

The next day, Dean helped me make a paper-bag mask to wear over my head, because I couldn't cut the eyes and mouth holes properly with my broken hand.

We sat on the couch watching a horror movie. He looked over at me. "You know, I actually prefer this look for you," he said. "I think brown is your color."

I pinched him on the arm.

"Ah! Don't touch me! I don't want the hiv."

Mom came into the room. "She doesn't have HIV, Dean."

"I don't?"

"No. I just got off the phone with the lab. You tested negative for all STIs."

"All of them? Everything? You're sure?"

"Yes," she said.

I put my paper-bag head in my hands and cried.

"Isn't that a good thing?" Dean said.

"No!" I yelled. "No one knows what's wrong with me!"

"Maybe you were bad, and now you're being punished for your sins," Dean said.

"Dean. Abby's not bad. You're a good girl, Abby. None of this is your fault," Mom said.

"No. He's right. I'm bad. I'm a bad person. I deserve this."

"Don't say that. You're a wonderful person."

"No I'm not, Mom," I sobbed. The paper bag was getting all damp inside from my tears. "I'm mean. I was mean to ugly people. And fat people. And losers. Dean's right. I'm being punished!"

Dean nodded. "It's true, Mom. It's God's will."

"Enough of this nonsense," Mom said. "We're going to find out what's wrong. And you're going to get better. That is all."

We all turned to look at the TV; a pretty blonde girl screamed and screamed and screamed as chunks of blood and viscera splattered across the wall behind her.

On top of all this, I was also recovering from a concussion. Which is, by definition, brain damage. Don't worry, Dean had a field day with this one.

So when you're recovering from a concussion, your brain does strange things. I couldn't really read. The words would get all messed up on the page and nothing made sense. And I could only watch TV for an hour or so at a time before my brain started to hurt. For a couple of weeks, I couldn't string sentences together and was stuttering all the time. I spent most of my time on the couch wrapped in my blankets, getting abused by Dean while he played video games.

"What does that say?" I looked at the red words on the TV screen, blurring and blending together.

He looked over at me. "It says 'Player One. Start.'"

"Oh."

"I guess cheerleading really brought out your inner moron," Dean said.

"Shut it."

"I mean, we always knew you were a little dumb, we just didn't know you were *this* dumb."

"Do you want to die?"

"In real life or in the game?"

"Life."

"Eventually, yes," he said.

"How about today?"

"Today's not good for me."

"Then sock a stuff in it."

He laughed. "I'll get right on that."

It took about a month and a half for me to be able to read, speak and walk properly again. But it seemed like decades. My spots didn't clear up, my joints ached and my face looked like a rotten cauliflower. Mom and Dad had talked with our family doctor, Dr. Jamieson, and together they'd decided that the best thing for me would be to go back to school after spring break, keep doing my normal routine as best as I was able, in order to avoid the major depression I was already inside of. I have absolutely NO IDEA how they thought that going to school looking the way I did could possibly *help* me in any way. And trust me, I fought with everything I had not to go. I even threatened to run away and join the Church of Scientology, which would be freaky as hell, obviously. But at least I'd have Tom Cruise to comfort me.

"Abby," Dad said. "This is your senior year. Your grades matter now more than ever. If you miss too much school, you won't be able to get into a good college. You might not be able to get into any college."

"I don't care about that," I said.

"Of course you do, you've always said you wanted to go away to college. You said you wanted to study acting."

Beside him, Mom nodded vigorously. "That's what you've always said, honey."

"Well, obviously that's never going to happen now," I said, pointing to my face.

"Never say never," Mom said. "We don't know how our lives are going to turn out. We have to keep our options open."

"But—"

"Abby," Dad said, "you're four months away from your high school graduation. Do you really want to quit school now, when you're so close?"

"Yes!"

"Well, too bad," he said. "I'm not letting you."

"*DAD!*"

"You'll thank me one day," he said.

"I won't do it. I can't go back. I can't go to school looking like this."

"Abby," Dad said. "Sometimes we just have to be brave."

I started to cry and they both gave me a hug and told me

they loved me. I wanted to tell them that I hated them for sending me back to school, but I was crying too hard to speak.

When school started again after the break, I went back. You think it's hard having acne and braces and a stupid-looking haircut? Try being a high school leper.

M arla and Liz came running up to me while I stood in front of my locker. I was trying to remember the combination to my lock. Marla's auburn hair glinted in the sunlight that poured through the windows. Somehow, she had gotten prettier, while I, well, I had become Jabba the Hutt. "Oh my God, Abby?" Liz covered her mouth with her hands. Liz had cut her hair super short, dyed it a mahogany color and wore a gold hoop in the side of her nose. She looked a lot different. She looked great.

"Hi," I said.

They didn't say anything. They just stared at me, mouths open. Other kids were staring too. I wished I could dissolve into the floor. *Maybe I should just get inside my locker and stay there until the last bell*, I thought. *I could probably fit, if I took out all my binders and textbooks.*

"Abby . . ." Liz said. "What happened to you?"

"I don't know. Nobody knows. I've seen a bunch of doctors. I've had blood tests and allergy tests and piss tests and no one knows anything."

"Oh my God," Liz said.

Finally, I got the right combo and opened my locker. The first thing I saw was the row of locker mirrors I had lined up inside the door so that I would have a full-length mirror in my locker. I shuddered. I was wearing a black ball cap, and a shitload of foundation to hide as much as I could, but Dean was right, my face looked like a three-day-old pizza. I'd had all my casts removed a few weeks before and I could feel Marla and Liz staring at the pale, wrinkled skin of my hands as I gathered my books.

"Are you okay?" Marla said.

I looked at her. I looked down at myself, then back at her. "I don't know," I whispered.

"Jesus," Marla said under her breath. Then the first bell rang.

"We gotta go, Abby," Liz said. They began backing away.

"Okay. See you at lunch?" I said.

"Yep," Liz called over her shoulder as she and Marla half-walked, half-ran down the hall. I slammed my locker and went to the girls' bathroom where I locked myself in a stall and cried for the entire first period.

It took everything I had to go to my next class, English, where I sat beside Leanne Sarsgaard. Leanne was also on the cheerleading squad. She had violet contacts and the longest legs in town.

"Hey, Abby," she said as I sat down.

"Hi," I said, pulling my cap lower.

"Did you have a good break?" She smiled at me.

"Yeah, whatever."

"Hey," she said, "I heard you got AIDS, is that true?"

"No," I said.

"Okay," she said. "I was just wondering because I know you were with Chad a while ago, and then he and I got together over spring break, and I was just wondering if I should get tested. Do you think I should get tested?"

"I don't know," I said.

"Do you think Chad gave it to you?"

"Gave what to me?"

"AIDS."

"I DON'T HAVE AIDS!"

Of course, that was the moment that Mr. Wilkes walked in and the whole room got quiet, so everyone heard me.

"That's good news, Ms. Furlowe," Mr. Wilkes said, nodding. The class tittered. "Okay, welcome back, people. Please take out your books. We're looking at Hamlet's soliloquy today."

I looked over the famous speech while my eyes blurred with tears. *Not to be, Hamlet. Not to be. There is no more question. There are no more reasons to be.*

I didn't know if I was the kind of person who could kill myself, but some things are worse than dying.

At lunch I got fries and a Coke and went to sit with Marla and Liz at our usual table. I set my tray down beside Marla's. She looked up at me, then quickly looked away.

"Hey," I said.

They said hi to me then stared at me while pretending not to. It was weird.

"How was your spring break?" I said.

"Sucked," Liz said.

"Probably not as bad as mine did," I said.

"Yeah." She looked down at her sandwich.

"So what do the doctors think it is?" Marla said.

"I might be dying. I don't know," I said.

"Oh my God! Abby!"

"That might be preferable to this actually," I said.

They stared at me some more as I tried to eat.

"*What?*" I said.

They both looked down. Then at each other. "It's just . . ." Liz said.

"It's just that we're not used to seeing you like this," Marla said.

"You're usually more . . . upbeat," Liz said.

"Ugh." I put my head down on the table. "I'm a hideous beast. What am I going to do?"

They looked at each other. Then back at me.

"I used to feel really ugly before I got my braces off," Liz said. "I hardly even smiled for three years."

I lifted my head. "This is *nothing* like having braces, so don't even try to compare it to that," I said.

"Sorry."

"You'll get through this, Abby," Marla said. "You'll be back to your old self again in no time."

"How do you know?"

She bit her lower lip. "And, hey, in the meantime, there's always makeup," she said.

"Do you have any idea how much makeup I'm wearing right now?" I pointed to my face. "It doesn't help!"

"Abby—"

"Okay, it helps a little bit, but not enough."

"What about plastic surgery?" Liz said.

Marla elbowed her in the ribs.

"Ow! It was just an idea. Or, or, what about, like, those Mission Impossible masks that look like a real face? You could get one of those made, like how your face used to be."

I put my forehead back down on the table. "I just wish I didn't have to go to school," I said. "I wish no one would see me like this."

One of them patted my arm. I'm not sure who because I had my eyes closed. Then Liz said, "Abby, sorry, but we really have to go."

"What?" I sat up. "Why?"

"Yearbook committee meeting."

"Yearbook? Since when do you care about the stupid yearbook?"

"Turns out Liz has a natural flair for photography," Marla said. "And Nate Russell spends an awful lot of time in the darkroom."

Liz grinned.

"Plus," Marla said, "people on the yearbook committee get to select and edit the photos that go in, so it's pretty much guaranteed that there won't be any bad, embarrassing pictures of us in there."

I nodded. "That's pretty smart, actually," I said.

"Right?"

"Promise me that you'll only use old photos of me, from before. Nothing from how I look now."

"Of course," Marla said.

"I don't want people to remember me like this."

"They won't," Liz said. "They'll only remember your profound hotness."

"Promise," I said.

"Totally."

Marla nodded.

"We should go," Liz said.

I sighed.

They stood up and gathered their things.

"I'll text you later," Marla said.

Liz waved as they walked away.

The cafeteria was noisy and full of students, and I had never felt more alone.

I ate my fries like a slow, dumb cow. I tried not to think about anything. It hurt too much to think about anything. My friends had moved on. They didn't need me anymore. Maybe they never had. My heart lay shattered inside my chest.

"Scabby Abby eats lunch alone now?" Dean sidled up to me.

"Don't call me that," I said.

"What should I call you? Princess Pus-face?"

"Fuck off."

Dean chuckled and stole one of my fries. Because my brother's a dumbass, he failed fourth grade, which is why we were in the same grade even though he's a year older than me.

"Hey," he said, "I heard Mom and Dad talking about going to Mexico for their anniversary. We should have a party."

Normally, I would've been all over that. I loved having parties. And we'd had some killer parties in the past. But everything was different. No one would want to make out with me; that was guaranteed.

"I don't know," I said. "I'm not—"

"Aw, c'mon, Abs. This is just what you need. It'll cheer you up," Dean said. "We can get a keg. It'll be great."

"When are they going?"

"Two weeks from now," he said. "As long as you don't get any worse."

I nodded.

"Don't get any worse, Ab."

"I'll try."

"No, try not. Do or do not. There is no try."

"Whatever, Yoda."

He did another Yoda impression. We sat together for the rest of lunch, and he made stupid jokes and told me a bunch of gossip that he was probably making up. Usually I wanted to be as far away from Dean as possible, but that lunch hour, I was so, so glad that he was sitting right beside me.

We all ate dinner together that night. Dad made his famous spaghetti and meatballs.

"How did it go at school today, Abby?" Dad asked.

I glared at him. "How do you think? I look like a freak."

"Abby," Mom said.

"What? It's true!"

She shook her head.

"Mom," Dean said. "It's true."

"See!"

"Did you go to all your classes?" Dad asked.

"Almost."

"Did you see your friends?"

I sighed and pushed a meatball around on my plate. I'd been checking my phone all night. Marla hadn't texted and neither had Liz. They probably wanted nothing to do with me. And why should they? I'd only rain on their pretty parade. "I don't think I have any friends anymore."

"That's not true," Dad said. "We're your friends."

"Dad! Come on. You're not my friends. You're my family."

"Same thing."

"No. No, it's not the same thing. Those are two different things. That's why there are different words for them. Because they're different things."

"Well, I can hang out with you. That's what you do with your friends, isn't it? Hang out?"

"Dad, I don't want to *hang out* with you," I said.

"Why not?" He looked hurt.

"Because you're my *dad*!"

He cleared his throat and concentrated on wrapping his spaghetti around his fork.

"What happened with your friends?" Mom asked.

"Just forget about it. I don't want to talk about it, okay?"

Mom sighed. "Things will get easier, Abby."

"The whole school thinks I have AIDS."

"You don't have AIDS," Mom said.

"*I* know that."

"*How was your day, Dean*?" Dean said. "Fine, thanks for asking."

"Sorry, Dean," Mom said. "Why don't you tell us about your day?"

"Well, I got asked about a billion times if Abby has AIDS. Most of the time, I said no."

"Dean!"

"Just kidding. About fifty percent of the time I said no."

"Dean!"

He laughed.

"You didn't," I said.

"No," he shook his head. "I didn't."

"Good."

He shrugged. "I told them you have syphilis."

I flew at him, swinging. Dad had to pull me off him. He sent us both to our rooms for the rest of the night. I wasn't sorry. I wished I'd hurt him. I should've stabbed him with my fork. Or my knife.

The next morning, I wouldn't talk to Dean. I wouldn't even look at him.

At lunch I walked into the cafeteria alone holding my tray. I passed the tables of geeks and mouth-breathers I had shunned since junior high. They glared and snickered at me, whispering to each other and shifting so that it would be clear there was no room at their table for me. I passed the table of fat girls: Larissa, Tracy and Heather. Also known as Lard Ass, Tubby and Heifer. They glanced up at me, shook their heads pityingly, and went back to their food. I passed the table of acne-plagued math geeks, people I had only ever been fake-nice to in case I needed to copy their calculus notes or physics homework. Brian Tate moved his backpack off the seat beside him and smiled up at me, his mouth a gleaming pocket of metal. His zits oozed as I stared at him, trying to decide if I'd really sunk this low, if this was where I belonged now.

Then, Jordan Lee swooped into the spot. "Hey, guys," he said in his nasally ten-year-old's voice. "What's the haps?"

Brian gave me a friendly shrug and I moved on. I walked to the farthest corner of the room, to the table reserved for total social rejects, and sat by myself while I pretended to read *Hamlet*. Dean didn't come sit with me. I kept an eye out for Marla and Liz but I didn't see them. I had texted them to meet me at my locker before lunch.

They didn't.

They didn't even look at me or say hi to me in the halls when we passed each other between classes. They looked right through me. Like I didn't even exist.

I was devastated. Obviously.

"Hey, Abby."

I jumped a little as Dustin Lorimer sat down beside me. I shielded the side of my face so he wouldn't see the crusty pink bumps around my hairline.

"Oh, hey, Dustin. How's it going?" I said.

We talked a little about spring break and what he had done (gone skiing up in Whistler and stayed up there in a cabin with his family), what I had done (recovered from several bodily injuries and a brain injury on account of my fall).

"Oh, yeah, I heard about that," he said.

"I was in a coma for sixteen days," I said.

He asked me what that was like and I told him. I didn't know why he was being so nice to me. I kept expecting him to stand up and point at me and yell *FREAK!* But he never did.

"How are you feeling?" he asked.

"I've been better," I said.

He nodded. "It looks like you still have some scrapes from the fall," he said, pointing to his own cheek.

I looked down. "Those aren't from the fall."

"Oh," he said.

I looked back up at him. He had such kind eyes. The color of Werther's Originals.

He looked at a spot on the table where someone had carved A.L. + W.S. inside a heart. He traced the heart with his finger. "My sister was sick," he said, nodding. "Nobody knew what it was for a long time. She kept getting misdiagnosed, misdiagnosed, meanwhile, she got worse."

"What did she have?" I asked.

"Crohn's disease," he said.

"Oh."

He nodded.

"Did she have to get surgery?"

"No. Surgery doesn't cure it. There is no cure."

"Oh," I said, feeling like an idiot. "That sucks."

He nodded.

"Is she alright, though?"

"She has a lot of pain. But I think she'll be able to get it under control. She's not supposed to drink is the thing."

"Oh."

"Yeah. But she does, once in a while, and then it flares up really bad and so . . ." He shrugged. "I don't know."

"How did they finally find out what she had?" I said.

"They did a biopsy of her colon, I think."

"Is that when they scrape a little piece off and then study it under a microscope?"

"I think so, yeah."

"Hm," I said. Then the bell rang.

"Well, I'll see you around," Dustin said. He gave me a small smile and took off. It was a pity smile, I was pretty sure of that.

No one had ever really given me a pity smile before. *I* was usually the one giving them out. I promised myself that when I got better, *if* I got better, I wouldn't do that anymore.

I skipped the next period and called my mom at work. She's the manager of an office supplies store downtown.

"Hello?"

I could hear the photocopier running in the background.

"Mom. Have I had a biopsy?"

"A biopsy?"

"Yeah."

"I don't think so."

"I need one. Right away. Maybe of my colon."

When I got home, I texted Marla and Liz: WTF???!!!???
    Liz texted back: Sorry. Really busy with yearbook and studying.
    So you can't even say hi to me in the hall???
    Sorry, Abby.
    Marla didn't text back at all.

Mom booked me in for a biopsy and I had it a few days later. Dr. Neal scraped some cells from my arm and some from my leg and some from the inside of my nose. He gave me a nod and said the lab would call when the results were in.

School sucked more than anything has ever sucked before in the history of the world. I hated myself and the way I looked and the way everyone looked at me, or didn't look at me. I felt bad for all the kids who had lived their whole lives ugly. It was a terrible way to go through the world. People looked right through you. Or immediately away. Good-looking people have so many more advantages. And they don't even realize it because things have always been that way for them. People really give them the benefit of the doubt. And all of the other benefits too. It's so unfair, there should be a law against it. No discrimination against uglies. But then people would have to identify as ugly. And that would be a whole other thing.

Later that week, I came home early from school because I just couldn't stand it anymore. When I walked into the house, Dean was on the couch making out with someone.

"Well, well, well," I said. "What do we have here?"

They both turned to look at me. And the person beneath him was a boy.

It was Aaron Forsythe.

They both had their shirts off. Dean stood up and put his shirt back on. He was clumsy and soft. His face flushed scarlet. Aaron sat up, all casual, buckled his studded belt, and said, "Oh, hey, Abby."

I started laughing. I'm not sure why. It wasn't funny. I think, sometimes, people laugh when they get a real surprise. That was a real surprise.

Dean coughed into his hand. "What are you doing home?" he said.

"Um, I live here?" I said.

Aaron reached for his pack of cigarettes on the coffee table and lit one.

"You can't smoke in here," I said.

Aaron just stared at the wall like he hadn't heard me. He blew smoke rings that floated toward the ceiling like weightless sugar doughnuts. Dean stared at the pack of cigarettes. Then he took one out and stuck it behind his ear. "C'mon, Aaron," Dean said. He started walking toward the screen door in the kitchen. Aaron looked sidelong at me and then at Dean, then got up and followed Dean. They went out to the backyard, slamming the screen door behind them.

I laughed again, shook my head and went up to my room. I lay on my bed and stared at the ceiling, wondering how many other things I didn't know about Dean. I wondered if I would tell my parents. And I wondered who else knew besides Aaron.

A while later, there was a knock on my bedroom door. I jolted awake. I had dozed off staring at the glow-in-the-dark stars stuck to my ceiling, trying to decide if they were nerdy or cool.

Dean stepped inside my room. "It's dinner," he said.

I rubbed my face. It was itchy and hot. My left eyelid felt scaly. I covered it with my palm for a moment.

Dean's eyes flicked from the edge of my bed to me. "Ab," he said.

"What?"

"Are you going to say anything?"

"Yeah. I'm going to say a lot of things. I know a lot of words," I said. "Some in Spanish too."

"No, I mean . . . You know."

"No. What, Dean?"

"C'mon, you know what I'm talking about."

"What? That you're gay?"

Dean blinked hard. "I'm not."

"You're not gay?"

He shook his head.

"So. Then . . .What? You're bisexual?"

He pressed his lips together.

"Come on, man!" I said. "You can't even make up your mind about who you want to sleep with? *Pick one!*"

"Abby—"

"What? What do you want, Dean? You want me to tell you that it's okay to screw Aaron on our couch? It's not okay. It's not okay to screw anyone on our couch. Guy. Girl. Donkey. No! *Nobody!* I have to sit there! Now where am I going to sit? It's gross! You're gross!"

"You're one to talk," he said. "Have you looked in a mirror lately?"

I picked up a glass on my bedside table and whipped it at his head. He ducked and it shattered against the wall.

He opened the door to leave. "Just keep it to yourself, okay?"

"Why should I?"

"Because," he said. "You're my sister."

Then he left, and I rolled over and cried into my pillow.

That night at dinner, Mom and Dad announced that they were going to some fancy-schmancy all-inclusive resort in Mexico for their anniversary. They had been married for twenty years, which was longer than my entire lifetime and impossible to imagine.

Mom stretched her arm across the table and squeezed Dad's hand. "We'd planned on going for two weeks," she said. "But I don't feel good about leaving you guys for that long, now that Abby's . . ."

"Abby will be fine, Mom. Go, enjoy yourself. You kids deserve it!" Dean said.

I stared at my plate.

"No," Dad said. "We're going for a week. That's enough." He smiled at Mom and she smiled back. They weren't happy smiles.

Dean cleared his throat. "And when were you planning on going?"

"This Friday," Dad said.

"Absolutely no parties while we're gone," Mom said.

"Of course not!" Dean said.

"I mean it, Dean," said Mom. "Auntie Karen's coming by to check on you and she'll tell me everything."

"Great," Dean said.

Auntie Karen is Dad's younger sister. She's a documentary filmmaker. Last time she had come to check on us while Mom and Dad were away, she bought us a case of beer, so her swinging by wasn't too much of a threat.

"Did the lab call today?" I said.

"No, sweetie," Mom said. "Dr. Neal said they probably wouldn't have the results until sometime next week. It could even be the week after that, depending on how backed up they are."

I nodded.

"And if anything happens while we're away and you need us to be here, you just call and we'll be on the next flight home, okay? That's no problem."

"Okay," I said.

I could hear the clock in the hall ticking. I was still hungry, but I didn't want to eat anymore. My food suddenly looked revolting. The pork chop especially.

"You're going to get better, Abby," Mom said. "You might not believe it now, but you will."

"This too shall pass," Dad said, nodding.

I wondered who they were trying to convince. Me or themselves.

Dean had invited a whole schwack of people to the party at our house Saturday night. I texted Marla to invite her and she wrote back: Sorry. Can't make it this Saturday. Have fun :)

The smiley-face was the worst.

Liz said: Have to babysit.

Yeah, right. She *never* babysat on a Saturday night if there was a party. She always said that having a rich social life was more important than having extra spending money.

I sat on my bed and stared at my phone. I thought about inviting Dustin, but I figured he would probably be there anyway, since he was a friend of Aaron and Aaron was my brother's boyfriend. Or something. I hoped that Jude and Carrie wouldn't come. And I also hoped that *nobody* would come. It was too hard for me to have people see me now. They used to smile when they saw me, strangers too. Guys were constantly checking me out. Now, people looked away or, worse, stared, and sometimes pointed. Just being alive was humiliating. I so badly wanted things to be like how they were before. I wanted to be beautiful again. I wanted my friends back. I had gone from being one of the hottest girls in school to one of the ugliest people in Texas, and maybe all of the United States, in a matter of months. It was devastating. Obviously.

Dean wasn't what I would call popular, but he knew everybody, and everybody kind of liked him. Or at least tolerated him. Or thought he was funny. I don't know. He was a jackass and he knew it. For some people, that kind of person is easy to be around because they never pretend to be something they're not. They don't pretend to like you when they actually don't. You *know* they don't like you because they don't like anybody. They're not fake. Or, it's a different kind of fake. I'm not sure.

Saturday afternoon was difficult. I went back and forth between being excited that we were having a party and trying to decide what to wear, to feeling like a hideous beast and deciding to stay locked in my room all night where no one could see me. I was beyond the help of makeup by this point. Only a full face-mask would save me, and it was too late to tell everyone it was a masquerade party and it would be too freaky for me to be the only one wearing a mask. Although I did consider wearing this old Phantom of the Opera mask that Mom had in her bottom drawer. But it creeped me right out when I tried it on and looked in the mirror, so I put it back. My lips were puffier than any Botox botch job you've seen, and I had bumpy red-and-white patches all along my hairline, behind my ears and a big oozy one on my left cheek. There were a bunch of scaly patches on my feet, legs, arms and hands, but I could keep those covered up easily enough.

I tore through my closet, pulling out everything with a hood or high collar. Dean burst into my room as I was trying on an old striped turtleneck.

"Hey! Knocking? Ever heard of it?"

"Abby." Dean walked in and grabbed my phone off my dresser, held it out to me. "You need to invite some of your girlfriends or else this is going to be a total sausage party."

"Isn't that what you want?"

"Abby! Come on!"

"Well? Isn't it?"

"For one, it's none of your business, okay, so you can just forget about what you saw the other day. And for two, nobody likes a party with just guys. It's weird. It's like a golf tournament or something."

"What, you don't want a hole in one?"

"Abs! Come on! Call your bitches!" He shoved the phone into my hand.

I stared at it.

"You know, the redhead and the short one you always hang around with."

"They're not coming," I mumbled.

"Well, maybe that's because you haven't *called* them!"

I shook my head.

Dean stared at me.

Tears welled up in the corners of my eyes. I shrugged and threw the phone on my bed.

"Because of . . ." He pointed to his face.

I nodded.

"Those little *bitches*."

I nodded.

"Do you want me to beat them up?"

"Yeah." I stepped into my closet so he wouldn't see my face. I was about to crumble. My best friends in the whole world had abandoned me when I needed them most. I had always thought that it would be a boy who broke my heart. But I was wrong.

People started showing up around nine. At first I stayed in my room but kept the door open so I could hear. I couldn't hear very well because of all the voices mixing together and the music on top of that. But if I sat right outside my door, I could peer over the banister and see what was going on and hear a little better. I wanted to go downstairs in the worst way, but there were so many people down there, people who knew me, knew how I was before, and I would've been ashamed to be around them. To have them see me like that. It made me sick to my stomach to think of them looking at me, pointing at my face, whispering about me once I turned my back. I couldn't bring myself to go downstairs, as much as I wanted to.

Nobody even asked where I was, even though most of the people there knew I was Dean's sister, knew it was my house too. It was like I didn't even exist anymore. It was like I was a big ugly smudge on someone's notebook that they had gone ahead and erased. These were the beautiful people; I was dead to them now.

At one point I really had to pee. I knew that people had been coming upstairs to use the bathroom; there was even a lineup for it at one point. I *so* did not want to run into anyone but finally I couldn't hold it anymore. I bolted to the bathroom and locked the door behind me. I peed, washed my hands, and then, in case I saw anyone on my way back to my room, I put an avocado face-mask on, spreading the green goo over everything but my lips and eyes. I opened the bathroom door a crack and peered out. Nothing. Then I opened it wider and stepped out, right into Dustin Lorimer's chest. I let out a little shout and he laughed in surprise, catching me by the shoulders. "We've got to stop meeting like this," he said.

"Hey, Dustin."

"You alright?"

"Yeah. You just startled me is all."

"Sorry," he said.

"It's okay."

"Nice, um . . ." He pointed to his face.

"Oh, yeah. It's very hydrating. Would you like to try some?"

He smiled. "Maybe some other time," he said.

"Alright. We can arrange that." I grinned at him, suddenly bold, since my face was covered in avocado and the lights were dim.

He asked me how I was doing and why I wasn't joining the party.

"I'm not feeling that well," I said and coughed into my sleeve.

"That's too bad. Missing your own party."

"Yeah, well, it's more of a facial-mask and mani-pedi night for me."

He looked confused.

"Um, manicure-pedicure?" I waved my fingernails at him, my chipped bronze polish catching the light.

"Right," he said. "Gotta stay on top of that stuff."

"Totally."

"But you should come downstairs. Even just for a bit. I think the beer pong's started. That's your game, isn't it?"

I did kick ass at beer pong. "I really can't," I said. "I'd like to. But I can't."

He nodded. "Okay. Well . . ." He gestured to the bathroom door.

"Right. It was good to see you, Dustin."

"You too, Abby. Hope you're feeling better soon."

"Thanks," I said. "Have a good night."

"I already have," he said.

We smiled at each other. Then I went back to my room and sat with my back against the door, wishing I could go downstairs. Wishing I was the kind of person who didn't care what she looked like, didn't care what other people thought of her. But I did, I did.

I hung out for a while in my room, painted my toenails black, then crept back out to the landing to listen to the party. Around midnight, it started pouring rain. It was, like, buckets and buckets of rain hitting the roof and the windows. There was lightning and thunder too. I could hear people saying it was just like Tropical Storm Allison, but nobody there could probably even remember Allison since we were all babies when it happened and some people at the party hadn't even been born yet. I heard Dustin say that he was going to get his car to high ground so it didn't float away, then he left and a bunch of other people did too, probably to do the same thing. Dean yelled after them, "Don't go! Don't leave! We'll survive this together! We've got to stick together! We'll build a raft!"

He took off his belt and waved it over his head. "We can use this!" He was super drunk and being even more obnoxious than usual.

Looking through the banister, I could see Aaron on the couch, macking on a petite brunette junior who had just transferred to our school from Calgary. I watched Dean watching Aaron. Aaron put his arm around the girl's shoulders and she snuggled into him. Dean stared at them and took another drink. He was drinking Wild Turkey, straight from the bottle.

The party dragged on and on. If I had actually been down there, it probably would've gone by fast, but since I couldn't go downstairs or talk to anybody, it felt never ending. The lights flickered for a moment when a big crash of thunder thudded through the house. Some girls screamed. I hoped that the power would go out because then it would be so dark that no one could see me and then I could go downstairs and party with everybody. But the lights never went out for more than a millisecond. Jason Redpath and a tall girl I didn't know came upstairs, probably looking for a place to make out, but I scooted back into my room and shut the door before they could see me and moved my chair up against the doorknob.

Mom and Dad wouldn't let us have locks on our bedroom

doors because they said it wasn't safe. *What if something happened to you? How would we get in?* But at that moment, I wanted nothing more than to be locked inside the sanctuary of my room, away from every pretty, happy person at that party, away from the whole world. I didn't want anyone to come in. Ever.

I lay down on my bed and closed my eyes. I must have dozed off for a while because when I woke up, the rain had stopped and the only sound was a CD skipping on Mom and Dad's ancient stereo downstairs. I opened my door a crack and looked out. I couldn't see anyone so I stepped out onto the landing and peeked over the banister. The rosy light of dawn seeped through the windows. A guy with no pants on was passed out on the couch; a blonde girl with huge boobs was asleep in the rocking chair, her mouth hanging open; and Aaron and the Canadian brunette were wrapped in a blanket on the floor. I tiptoed down the hall to Mom and Dad's room and pushed the door open with my finger. No one was in there. Thank God. Then I checked Dean's room. It was also empty. I went to his window and looked out over our backyard. The lawn was a lake. It had rained *a lot*. Some people had parked in the back alley behind our house but I didn't see Dustin's car anywhere. I hoped it was okay. He drove a hybrid car: half-electric, half-gasoline. Some guys made fun of him for it, called him a tree hugger and crap like that, but I thought it was pretty cool. I stared out the window. A sodden black cat scrambled over the top of our neighbor's fence. I watched as it shook itself off, spraying spirals of water into the morning air.

Out of the corner of my eye, I saw a patch of something red moving just inside the door of our shed. It seemed to be flailing, convulsing. I flashed on a memory of Dean waving his belt over his head. He had been wearing his red skate shoes. I got a queasy feeling in my stomach. I felt weak and sick. Something was wrong with the red thing, whatever it was.

I moved through the house like I was walking through Jell-O. Everything around me was slow and thick. Then I was standing in the shed.

Dean lay propped against a bag of soil, covered in vomit. His face was a pasty green. Pale chunks coated his mouth and chin and there were piles of puke on the ground beside him. His shirt and jeans were encrusted in what looked like pink oatmeal. The shed reeked of rotten milk, acidic orange juice and pee. Dean had pissed his pants! Loser! I covered my nose with my arm.

"Dean." I nudged him with my foot. "Get up. You're a mess." I nudged him again, a little harder. "Dean!"

He didn't move.

I knelt down and pulled open his eyelids. His eyes were rolled back in his head. I slapped his face. Once, twice, three times, hard. Nothing. He didn't flinch. He didn't moan. He didn't move. "DEAN!!! WAKE UP!!!" I dug through the layer of puke on his neck to find his pulse. I couldn't feel anything. Then I watched his chest and belly and put the back of my hand in front of his nose. I couldn't feel anything. "Shit shit shit." I looked around. There was no one outside, no noises even. There was only the steady drip of water draining from the eaves. Everything was in slow motion. This was it. This was the moment of truth.

I had fantasized many, many times about killing my brother, or him being in an accident, about what it would be like to be an only child, life without Dean. I knew it would be peaceful. Serene, even. I stared at him for a moment. I hated him most of the time, but when it came right down to it, I actually did love him and I didn't want him to die. Not now, not ever.

I took out my phone. The battery was almost dead. I dialed 9-1-1, my hands shaking. I had just enough time to tell the operator I needed an ambulance and our address before my phone died.

Then I scooped the vomit out of Dean's mouth, pushed him onto his back and leaned over him to do CPR. I knew how to do CPR because I'd had about five training courses in it, between babysitter training, lifeguarding, cheerleading camp, my first aid course and learning it at school, I was pretty sure I could do it on a real life person, not just a plastic dummy.

I tilted Dean's forehead back to open the airway, plugged his nose and made a seal over his mouth with my own mouth, which is nothing like kissing so you can just stop thinking whatever you were thinking about me making out with my own brother. Ew. I gave him two breaths then started pumping hard and fast on his chest. *What is the song? What is that stupid song?* "Come on, Dean, what is the song?" I squeezed my eyes shut tight. *Come on. I know this.*

"Ah. Ha. Ha. Ha. Ha. Something, something," I whispered.

They say that if you pump someone's chest to the tune of that Bee Gees song, it's the right number of beats per minute to start the heart again. Disco saves lives. Who knew? I couldn't remember all of the words. But I knew some of them. And I sang along as I pushed on my brother's chest, again and again. "Now it's alright, it's okay, something something, other way. . . ." Pump. Pump. Pump. Pump. Two breaths. "Stayin' alive. Stayin' alive." I felt a sickening crack beneath my palms. I knew I had probably broken one of his ribs, but I didn't stop. I was going to keep doing it until he came back to life or I died, whichever came first.

After four rounds of CPR, Dean began to splutter and cough. Relief flooded over me in a hot wave. I rolled him onto his side and shoved him into a sitting position. I leaned him against the wall. "That's it. That's it, brother," I said. He vomited into his shirt. "Okay, well . . . that's okay," I said, nodding. He was breathing, that was the important part. I wiped my face with my shirt. He looked at me, drool running down his chin. His eyes were glazed and vacant.

"Can you hear me, Dean?"

He stared at me.

"Water. Do you want some water?"

He stared at me.

I ran into the house to get him a glass of water. The guy on the couch was stirring, and Aaron and Calgary were mumbling inside their blanket, but I didn't care who saw me now. I had just saved someone's life, everyone else was hungover. Clearly, I was dominating here.

I raced back out to Dean. I held the glass to his lips but he didn't take any water. He coughed and drooled some more. He smelled awful. I heard the sirens and ran out to the driveway. I led the two paramedics to the shed. They asked me a bunch of questions while they loaded Dean onto a stretcher. I told them I had found him about ten minutes ago, called them and then done four rounds of CPR, and he started breathing again on the fourth round. The bearded paramedic smiled. "Good job, kid. You just saved his life."

The other paramedic nodded. "Well done," she said. "You did exactly the right thing."

"Okay," I whispered, hugging my arms against my body. I didn't tell them that I had hesitated for a split second when I first found him lying there, helpless and unconscious. But maybe those are the kind of secrets you take to your grave.

"You want to sit up front or in the back?" the blonde paramedic asked. They had already loaded Dean into the back of the ambulance.

I looked at the house, then back to my brother. "I'll sit back here with him," I said, and climbed in. The two of them got in the back and banged the doors shut. The driver took off, sirens wailing. They hooked Dean up to some machines, put an oxygen mask on him and stabbed an IV into his arm.

"What's that?" I said.

"Epinephrine," said the bearded paramedic. "Brings his heart rate up."

"I think I broke his rib," I said. "Maybe more than one."

"Don't worry about that. It happens," he said. "You got his heart started again, that's the important part."

At the hospital, they put a tube in Dean's throat that was hooked to a breathing machine. Then they put another suction tube up his nose that threaded back into his throat and down into his stomach, so in case he threw up again it would suck out all the puke so he wouldn't choke on it.

Basically, they inserted an alcohol vacuum. Nasty. They also put him on an IV with fluids and electrolytes and all the junk he would need to recover.

I took out my phone a bunch of times to text Mom and Dad. But I always kept putting it away again. I'm not sure why. It seemed like we had made it through the worst of it. He was in stable condition. He was going to be okay. Their coming back from Mexico now couldn't possibly help anything. Plus, they'd be mad as hell that we'd had a party and gotten this far out of hand. Maybe I would never tell them. Maybe it would be another secret that Dean and I kept from them. I thought maybe, when we were old, like, thirty or something, and had moved out and gotten our own houses and everything, then we could tell them one time when we came to visit. And we could all sit around and laugh about it. About what a dumbass Dean had been. That seemed like a better time to tell them. Better than while Dean was being alcohol vacuumed. I looked at Dean, tubes running into his nose and mouth and arm. *You're an idiot*, I thought. *But I am so glad you're alive.* I brushed a tear off my cheek and blew my nose, then went to get a drink from the vending machine.

Around noon, I went home to have a shower and change my clothes. Everyone from the party had left, and of course no one had bothered to clean anything up. In the past, Marla and Liz had always helped me clean up after our parties. But that was before. There were cans and bottles and plastic cups and empty chip bags all over the place, and dirty smudges and footprints all over the floor. The house smelled like cigarette butts and stale beer and ass. I cranked the stereo and spent a few hours cleaning, then drove Mom's car back to the hospital. They were going to keep Dean overnight to monitor him.

"Okay," I said. "Call me when I can come and get him."

They kept him Monday night too. I skipped school Tuesday to bring him home.

"Hey, Ab," he said when I walked into his hospital room. His lips were white and cracked.

"Hey."

"Are you here to bring me home?"

I nodded.

"Great."

"Got a little problem though," I said.

"What?"

"The hospital bill."

"Oh."

"If we don't pay it now, it'll go to Mom and Dad, and then . . ."

"Right."

"Should we ask Auntie Karen?"

"No, no," Dean said. "That won't be necessary."

I looked at him.

"Did you bring my wallet?"

"Yeah." I took it out of my purse and handed it to him.

"Good." He pulled out his yellow bank card and held it out to me. "Savings. One, nine, nine, nine."

"Dean, it's going to be thousands of dollars—"

"It's okay."

A nurse came in then to discharge him. "Alrighty then," she said. "Let's get you ready to go, shall we?"

Dean nodded then turned to me. "Just go pay. I'll be out in a minute."

"Are you sure?"

"Yep."

"Okay." I went out to the reception desk, signed all the release forms and handed over his bank card. When I saw the amount being charged I held my breath, positive that the machine would beep, read *Insufficient Funds*.

But it didn't.

It went through.

My brother was rich. Somehow.

We got in the car. I was angrier than I thought I would be.

"Were you trying to kill yourself?"

"No." He shrugged. "I don't know."

"What's the matter with you?"

He stared out the window. "You wouldn't understand."

"Why? Because I'm straight?"

"No, because you're shallow."

I felt like I'd been kicked in the stomach. I knew he wasn't just teasing or saying it to be mean. He meant it. And the worst part was, I didn't even know if he was wrong or not.

We didn't talk for the rest of the ride home. When we got back in the house, I heated up a can of chicken noodle soup and made us some toast. We ate together at the table, which we would never normally do if Mom and Dad weren't there.

"This is good," Dean said.

"Campbell's."

He nodded.

We slurped our soup for a few minutes.

"Where did you get all that money?"

"Can we talk about something else?"

"Like what?"

"Like, are we going to tell Mom and Dad about this?"

"Depends," I said.

"On what?"

"Are you going to pull something like that again?"

He looked down at his hands. "It was an accident, Abby. I just drank too much, too fast on an empty stomach. It happens."

"Yeah, you know what else happens, Dean? People *die*."

He stared into his soup.

"You would've fucking *died* if I hadn't found you when I did. Then what?"

"Then . . . you'd finally have some peace and quiet . . . ? And a second closet for all your clothes?"

"Dean!" Tears stung my eyes. "This isn't funny!"

"Okay, okay. You're right. What do you want me to say? I'm sorry I scared you? I'm sorry I'm an idiot and thanks for saving my life?"

"That would be a start," I said.

"I didn't know that would happen, Abby. I really didn't."

"Well, it can't happen again," I said.

"Okay."

"Because what if I'm not around next time to find you, then—"

"I said *okay*."

"Alright then."

He stirred his spoon around in his soup. "So what about Mom and Dad?" he said.

"What about them?"

"Are you going to tell them?"

"Tell them what? That you're gay or that you tried to drink yourself to death?"

"I didn't—I'm not—"

"Whatever."

"So . . . ?"

"So, what?"

"So, are you?"

"I don't know, Dean. I don't want to ever have to see you like that again, I know that for sure."

"You won't."

I sighed. "If you can swear to me that you won't ever do anything like that again, I won't say anything about it to Mom and Dad. But if I even *suspect*—"

"Thank you," he said quietly.

"Promise me."

"Pinkie swear." He held his pinkie out to me and I hooked mine around his. We shook, but I couldn't feel it. I thought my hand was asleep. I flicked my wrist a few times and stretched my fingers back and forth. Dean looked at me, one eyebrow raised.

"Too much texting, I think. My hand goes numb sometimes. It's kind of weird."

"Maybe you just need a boyfriend," he said. "Then you could give your hand a rest."

My brother was back to his old self, for better or worse.

Auntie Karen came by the next day to check in on us. She brought us six doughnuts because, "Growing kids need doughnuts." She doted over me like a fake mom and held her hand against my forehead and asked me how I was feeling about a thousand times. It was kind of funny because Dean was the one who had just had the near-death experience, but she didn't even ask him how he was. She asked him how *school* was, which is not the same thing.

"Your mom and dad are really worried about you, Abby."

"Yeah," I said. "So worried they had to take off to Mexico for a week."

"They've had this trip planned for years, Ab. Don't hold it against them."

"No. It's fine. I get it."

"Aww." Dean made a big pouty-face at me across the table.

"Have your test results come back yet?" Auntie Karen asked.

I shook my head.

"When do you expect them?"

"Today? Tomorrow? Yesterday?" I said. "It's impossible to know. They're so vague."

She nodded. "It's always that way, isn't it?"

"I don't know," I said. "Nothing like this has ever happened to me before."

"Oh, sweetie." She leaned over to give me a sideways hug. She smelled like something citrusy, with peppermint mixed in. Her long brown hair fell into my face for a moment and I couldn't see. She kissed the side of my head then leaned back in her chair, looking at me with her head tilted to the side. I couldn't help it. I started to cry. Dean left the room.

"Oh, no. Abby. It's okay. Don't cry." She got up and got me a glass of water. "Here." She set it in front of me and I drank it between sobs. "What's wrong? Was it something I said?"

I shook my head. "I just feel so . . . ugly!" I spluttered. "Look at me. I'm hideous!"

"No you're not, Abby."

"You're just saying that. But it's not true." I folded my arms on the table and put my head on them.

"It *is* true because I know you and I know that inside you're a beautiful person."

"Arrgh!" I yelled into my arms.

"What?" She patted my back. "What is it, hon?"

"That just sounds so cheesy. And I don't even think *that's* true."

"I'm sorry," she said. "But you are a good person, Abby."

I lifted my head. "Yeah, but what if I'm not? What if I'm shallow and mean?" I wiped my nose on the back of my sleeve.

Auntie Karen stared at me, her eyes as blue and clear as beach glass. "Is that what you think?" she said quietly.

I nodded. Yes. No. "I don't know," I said. "Maybe."

The thing about Auntie Karen is that she's technically an adult, but she still seems an awful lot like a teenager. I'm not sure why this is. She doesn't have any kids of her own, so maybe that has something to do with it. She knew we'd had a party because she found a beer cap under her chair later that night. She held it up and raised an eyebrow at us.

"I wonder how that could've gotten there," Dean said.

Auntie Karen shook her head and flicked the cap into the trash. But we also knew that she wouldn't say anything about it to Mom and Dad. She could be counted on that way.

"I kind of feel like pizza and a movie tonight," she said.

"That's funny. You don't *look* like pizza and a movie," Dean said. "*Abby*, on the other hand . . ."

"Eat it, dick-breath," I said.

Dean gave me the finger.

"Hey, hey, hey," said Auntie Karen. "What's all this about?"

"This is about Dean being a capital D douche-bag twenty-four seven, three-sixty-five. Also, he sucks off guys."

Auntie Karen looked from me to Dean.

"You know," Dean said, "pizza and a movie sounds pretty good. As long as it's not some stupid chick flick."

Auntie Karen nodded slowly. Then she stood up. "No chick flicks, got it." She put on her leather jacket and grabbed her purse. "Should I pick up some beer?"

"*NO!*" Dean and I both yelled.

"Okay, okay." She backed down the hallway, hands in the air. "No beer. No chick flicks. No problem."

She came back with a large pepperoni pizza and a bottle of Coke and we found *Die Hard 2* on Netflix. The three of us sat on the couch and watched the movie while we ate all the pizza and drank all the Coke. Dean and Auntie Karen got into a contest to see who could burp the loudest. Dean won, but not by much.

There was nothing special about that night, nothing that stood out about it so much that I would remember every little detail. Except that I *do* remember everything about that night, because it was the last night I had of being a normal seventeen-year-old girl—if you could even call me that. It was the night before I found out I had leprosy.

Our home phone rang the next morning a little after 8:30 a.m. Dean and I looked at each other, then looked at the phone. I grabbed it off the wall while I poured milk on my Cheerios.

"Hello?"

"Hi, may I please speak to Miss Abby Furlowe?"

"This is Abby."

"Hi, Abby. This is Michelle calling from Diagnostic Laboratories."

"Yeah?"

"Your test results are in."

"Okay . . ."

"So you need to make an appointment to see your doctor to discuss them."

"Can't you just tell me?"

"Sorry. We can't give out results over the phone."

"Why not?"

"It's our policy."

"But . . . okay, so I have to make a doctor's appointment and take an afternoon off school, drive across town to go in and see him so that he can tell me? Instead of you just telling me right now on the phone?"

"That's right."

I sighed.

"Sorry," she said. "It's our—"

"Policy. Yeah, you said that."

"Dr. Jamieson has received your results. He'll be able to—"

"Can you just tell me one thing? Am I going to die? Do I have, like, six months to live or something? Because, I think I should find out as soon as possible if that's the case."

"I'm sorry. I don't actually know what the lab results are. All I know is that they've been sent to your doctor and you're to meet with him to discuss them. At your earliest convenience."

"That's the thing, though. It's *not* convenient."

"Well . . ."

"Could you text me my results? That would be convenient."

"No, I'm sorry. You need to make an appointment to see Dr. Jamieson," she said.

"Okay. Then. That is what I will do."

"Terrific."

"Super."

"Great. Well, take care, Miss Furlowe."

I hung up.

"Good news?" Dean said.

I rolled my eyes at him. He shrugged, then got up to get his stuff ready for school, leaving his dirty breakfast dishes on the table.

I drank an entire pint glass of orange juice without breathing. Then I called Dr. Jamieson's office. They'd had a cancellation that morning so there was a spot at 9:20 a.m. I skipped school and drove Mom's car to Dr. Jamieson's office. There was no way I could wait.

"Mycobacterium leprae," Dr. Jamieson said, staring at the paper on his desk. "Bacteria that causes leprosy. Also known as Hansen's disease." He looked up at me and winced.

My body felt like cold concrete. A dark, bottomless pit sucked me down into it. The mother of all migraines attacked my brain. I wanted nothing more than to vomit. I wanted to vomit across Dr. Jamieson's desk and all over Dr. Jamieson himself. A tiny little laugh escaped my mouth. But nothing was funny. Nothing would ever be funny again. I stared at my left hand on the arm of the chair.

"Will my fingers fall off?"

"No. But you will need to protect them from injury," Dr. Jamieson said. He kept talking but I wasn't listening anymore.

I had leprosy.

I was a leper.

There was nothing else to say.

The next thing I knew, I was sitting on my bed in my room. I don't really remember how I even got home from the doctor's office. I puked into my garbage can. Then I cried. I was hyperventilating, I smelled like vomit and I had leprosy. I don't know if life gets any worse than that. I curled around my pillow and cried until my head felt like it had been run over and my pillow was soaked with snot and tears. I willed a sinkhole to open up beneath our house and suck me down into it. I waited for a while to see if that, or some other fluke disaster, would happen to spare me from this misery. Nothing happened. I finally had to get up because I needed to pee. Then I went to find the phone number of the hotel Mom and Dad were staying at. I wanted my mom.

"Hello?"

"Mommy?"

"Hi, Abby. What's wrong, sweetie? What is it?"

I couldn't form words around the lump jammed in my throat. How could I tell her I had the worst disease known to humankind? I couldn't even breathe.

"You can tell me, whatever it is, Abby. You know you can tell me."

"I have leprosy!" I bawled into the phone.

"Narcolepsy?"

"No—"

"*That's* why you've been sleeping so much! You know, I used to work with a woman—"

"LEPROSY, Mom! *Lep*rosy."

"You . . . what?"

"I have leprosy."

Silence.

"*Mom!*"

"What did they say?" Her voice was very tiny and she sounded so far away.

"I'm a leper!"

"Oh, Abby. You're not a leper, honey."

"I'm pretty sure that's the definition of a leper. Someone who has leprosy. *I have leprosy.*"

"Oh, God. I'm sorry. I'm so sorry, Abby."

"YOU'RE SORRY!?" I started crying harder. It was a mad, manic crying now, the kind where it sounds more like laughter. My vision was so blurred with tears, I couldn't see. Finally I caught my breath and swallowed and found that I could speak again. "Mom?"

"Yeah, baby?"

"I don't know what to do."

"We're coming home tomorrow, Abby. We'll figure it out, okay? Whatever it is, we'll figure it out."

"Dr. Jamieson said I have to go to Louisiana."

"What? Why?"

"Because that's where the treatment center is. They're going to put me on drugs that kill the leprosy bacteria. But I have to live with a bunch of other lepers until the drugs start working!"

"Oh, Abby . . ."

"Is this real, Mom? Am I having a nightmare right now? You'd tell me, right? You'd wake me up—"

"Abby."

"WAKE UP!" I pinched my arm, hard. "WAKE UP. WAKE UP. WAKE UP."

"ABBY."

"What?"

"Take a hot bath. Make it as hot as you can stand it. Stay in it for twenty minutes. Then put on your pj's and get into bed. We'll be home tomorrow as fast as we can, okay?"

"Okay."

"I love you, sweetie. We'll get through this. Don't worry."

"You'll love me even though I'm a leper?"

"Of course I will. I'll always love you. No matter what."

"Okay." I was crying again now, but it was different, softer, barely there crying.

"Okay?"

"Okay," I whispered.

"See you tomorrow, Abby."

"Bye, Mom."

I hung up. Then I went to the bathroom and threw up again.

There's that expression, "It's not the end of the world." But sometimes, it actually is. This was one of those times. I was a teenage leper. My life was over. I died that day. A part of me did, anyway. And for as long as I live, I'll never be able to get it back. I'll never be able to say, "I didn't have leprosy. I was never a leper."

Someone out there reading this might say, "There are worse things." Maybe even you would say that. But I don't believe you.

I had to check in to the treatment facility in Baton Rouge, Louisiana, ASAP. Mom and Dad came home the next day, around noon like Mom had said, and we all cried together, except for Dad and Dean because guys don't cry apparently. But I'll bet you any money they cried afterwards. On their own. In private. Dad's eyes were all puffy and Dean's were pink and watery like Mom's, so I could tell.

Probably guys cry all the time, or at least, a lot more than people think they do, it's just that nobody sees them do it. Like a tree falling in the woods sort of thing.

I was up late that night. Super late. For some reason I was having trouble sleeping . . . Oh, right, I'd just found out I had leprosy and had to get shipped out of state to go take drugs that would kill the disease-bacteria living in my body. Talk about the vacation of a lifetime.

I got sucked into an Internet vortex looking at photos of people with leprosy and reading about leprosy and the treatment facility in Baton Rouge. I stared at the computer for so long, it felt like metal filings were being shoved into my eyeballs. I couldn't read any more. I closed my computer and went to get a drink from the bathroom. I saw that Dean's light was on, and because I was distracted, or I wasn't thinking, or a combination of the two, I opened Dean's door.

Dean was sitting at his computer, jerking off, with an open jar of peanut butter beside him and peanut butter all over his dick. There was another guy on his computer screen, an older guy.

"Jesus, fuck!" Dean saw me and jumped out of the chair. He turned off his monitor and grabbed a pillow and held it in front of him. "What do you want, Abby?"

"I, uh. Ha. I'm sorry."

"Okay, okay. Get out!"

"It's just . . ."

"WHAT?" Dean held the pillow to his crotch. He looked like Beaker the muppet.

I stifled a laugh. "What are you doing?"

"Just get out."

I left and got ready for bed, trying to erase that scene from my mind. That is something a sister should never see her brother doing. But as Dad would say, there are no mulligans in the game of life. I listened to music on my headphones and told myself it had never happened. I was in bed, almost ready to turn off my light when there was a rap at my door.

"Yeah?"

Dean peeked his head in. "See? Knocking. It's what people do," he said, tapping his fist against the door frame.

"Come on in, Jelly," I said.

"Don't even."

"PB, then."

"Shut it, leper." He was wearing plaid pajama pants and a gray T-shirt. He stood beside my bed with his arms crossed over his chest, looking awkward.

"What do you want?"

He eyed the end of my bed.

I scooted up and patted a spot for him to sit down. He hesitated, looked around. He sat at the edge of my desk chair, as if he couldn't stand for it to touch him. His eyes drifted over me, then he stared at the wall above my head.

"*What?*" I said. "What is it?"

"I'm a webcam boy."

"Uhhhh . . ." I said, laughing. "What do you mean?"

"You've heard of the Internet, right?"

"Shut up. Just tell me."

"So . . . people on the Internet pay to see me . . . you know. Do stuff."

"For real?"

He nodded.

"Whoa."

"I just got paid two hundred dollars for that."

"The peanut butter?"

He nodded. "Last week I was paid four hundred dollars to eat a cucumber."

"Naked."

"Well, yeah, I was naked, and I know it's kind of whacked, but four hundred bucks, Abby. I mean, it's not that hard to eat a cucumber."

"But what if next time they want you to do more than just eat it?" I said.

"I have my limits."

"Everyone has a price," I said.

"It's not like that."

"Okay, stop. Stop. You're nasty. I don't want to hear any more." I clamped my hands over my ears. "La-la-la-la."

"Listen. LISTEN. I've made enough to be able to move out this summer and afford all my own everything. A car too."

"And that's how you had enough to pay the hospital bill . . ."

He nodded.

"But isn't it . . . gross?"

He shrugged.

"Ick." I shivered. "I couldn't do it. Aren't the guys all old and creepy?"

Dean laughed. "Not always."

"So they, like . . ."

"What?"

"They tell you to do stuff and you do it?"

"Yeah. Well, there's a proposition and a negotiation that goes on."

"Wow."

"I mean, I won't do everything. I've said no to stuff before."

"I can't—"

"It's just until . . . I don't know why I'm telling you this. You can't tell Mom and Dad."

"Okay."

"Not ever."

"*Okay.*"

"Even when we're old."

"*Alright*," I said.

"It's just that it's so much money, you know? And it's pretty easy. Like, no one we know can pay for all their own stuff, right? Even if they do have a job. I mean, you have to work A LOT to be able to buy your own food and rent and furniture and TV and car and all that. Insurance. Gas. Who do you know that can afford all that?"

"On their own? Hardly anybody," I said.

"Exactly."

"So you, like, take Paypal, or what?"

"Yeah, Paypal."

"No way."

"It's true."

"I can't believe this."

"The numbers don't lie, baby."

"You're messed up."

"I've made fifteen grand in the last four months. You have leprosy. Who's winning here?"

I covered my face with my hands. "Good night, Dean."

"Sorry. I mean, I'm sorry that you have leprosy and that you have to go to Louisiana . . . I feel sorry for anyone who has to go to Louisiana, actually."

"Thanks."

"No, I'm serious. It stinks there. Especially in Baton Rouge."

"Whatever."

"They have a chemical plant there or something."

"So, is it, like, always the same guy or is it different guys, or what?"

"They're usually different, but I have my regulars."

"Jesus."

"Jesus isn't one of them, no."

"But you never meet them in person, right? I mean . . ."

"It's all from the comfort of my own room."

"Wow."

"Pretty easy, right?"

I stared at him. "Who else knows you're doing this? Does Aaron know?"

"No. No one knows. Just you. And if you tell anyone, I'll kill you."

"Christ, Dean."

"Some of them are actually really nice. I mean, we talk afterwards sometimes and . . ."

"Stop." I covered my ears. "I don't want to hear any more. For real this time."

Dean's face fell. "Fine. Whatever."

"Good."

He looked around my room. "You scared about tomorrow?"

I nodded.

He eyed my overflowing suitcase. "How long are you staying for?"

"I don't know," I said. "As long as I have to, I guess."

"You'll be living with other lepers, huh?"

"I guess."

"What if you get it from them?"

"I already have it, idiot."

"Yeah, but you could get it, like, twice as bad."

"I don't think it works that way." I picked at my nails.

"Okay, I've got something to cheer you up."

"What?"

"Why did they have to cancel the leper hockey game?"
I rolled my eyes. "Why?"

"There was a face off in the corner."

"Dean—"

"Okay, okay. What did the leper say to the prostitute?"
I shook my head.

"Keep the tip!"

"Dean! You're disgusting! Stop! Just get out!"

"You laughed! I saw you laugh a little bit!"

"Okay. Fine. Whatever. Just leave, alright?"

His smirk faded. "Alright. I might not see you tomorrow, so I guess I'll say goodbye now."

"Okay."

"So . . . goodbye." He stood up and looked like he wanted to hug me or pat my back or something. But he couldn't. He couldn't bring himself to touch me. I had leprosy. I was untouchable. He folded his arms across his chest and tucked his hands into his armpits. He nodded.

"Bye, Dean."

"Good luck down there."

"Thanks."

"Maybe when you get back we could take a trip into the city. I was thinking you could help me pick out some things for my new place. You know, like, house stuff that goes together and looks good. You've always been good with that interior design crap."

"Okay," I said. "Sure."

"Alright then. Well. Good night."

"Good night."

He closed my door and I was alone.

The next day, Mom and Dad drove me to the National Hansen's Disease Clinic at the Ochsner Medical Center in Baton Rouge, Louisiana. My hands vibrated in my lap. I sweat through my T-shirt and my cardigan. I chewed off all my nails. We had to stop four times so I could pee and once so I could throw up. It was the longest seven hours of my life.

The plan was for me to get checked in at the clinic, do all my tests, take my first round of pills and whatever else they wanted me to do there, then get on the special bus to Carville, the old leper colony, twenty miles away, where I was to stay during my treatment. *With other lepers.*

"But if it's really terrible in there, I can call, and you guys will come get me, right?"

Mom and Dad glanced at each other.

"*Right?*"

"You have to stay until the drugs take effect, Abby," Dad said.

"Says who?"

"The doctors, the specialists, the government, *us*."

Mom looked back at me.

"But what if it's awful and I can't stand to be there anymore? What am I supposed to do? Run away? Jump into a waterfall so they can't track me like Harrison Ford in *The Fugitive?*"

"No," Mom said. "You stay. Because that's the only way you're going to get better."

"But what about . . . what about . . . my life?" I stared out the window as we passed another bayou.

"This is your life, honey," Dad said. Then he turned up the radio and we listened to some old-timey blues. I watched out the window as swamps took over the land, and nobody said anything for about a hundred miles.

The people at the clinic were all pretty nice. They didn't have leprosy. Not the workers anyway. And they didn't call it leprosy. Not once. Hansen's disease, they called it. A lady with Harry Potter glasses checked me in and I filled out the forms she gave me. Mom and Dad sat on either side of me in the waiting room, looking awkward. Dad pretended to read email on his phone, and Mom kept asking me questions. How did I feel? Was I too hot? Was I too cold? Was I going to be sick again? Did I *think* I was going to be sick again? Did I have a headache? A fever? A sore neck? Did I bring my toothbrush? My homework? My bathrobe?

"Mom," I said.

"Yes?"

"Can we just not talk for a while?"

"Sure." She nodded, folded her hands in her lap. "Sure."

"Thanks."

A short while later, I was called in to see the doctor.

"Do you want me to come in with you?" Mom asked.

"Okay," I said.

We followed the Harry Potter lady down the hall. She opened the door of a little room for us. "Dr. Mike will be in shortly," she said.

Mom and I sat down on the faded pink chairs. There were a couple of old celebrity gossip magazines on a magazine rack. I reached for one, and then pulled my hand back. I didn't want to touch them. People with leprosy had touched them. I knew I already had it, but I didn't want to get it worse. Or get it again. Or whatever. Mom looked at me. She moved her mouth into some weird shape, which I guess was supposed to be a smile. Then there was a knock and Dr. Mike came in. He was around forty-five and had salt-and-pepper hair.

"Abby?" he said.

"Hi."

"Hello, I'm Dr. Mike." We shook hands. His eyes were the bluest shade of blue I'd ever seen. The kind of blue that pierces right into your heart.

"I'm Patricia, Abby's mom." Mom stuck out her hand to Dr. Mike.

He shook it and smiled briefly, the edges of his eyes crinkling. Then he washed his hands in the tiny sink, dried them on a paper towel, rolled it into a ball and tossed it into the garbage can. He cleared his throat and sat down across from us. Mom thought he was a babe, I could tell. She was blushing and fiddling with her hair.

"Abby," Dr. Mike said, turning back to me.

"Hi," I said again.

He nodded. "Hi."

"So . . ." I said.

"So. It's been confirmed that you have Hansen's disease. I know this must be really difficult news to accept, but you need to know that there *is* a cure and that your condition has not progressed to the point of permanent disfigurement. However, most of the nerves in your hands and feet have been destroyed and we must consider this to be a permanent disability."

I nodded and blinked away tears. Mom reached over and squeezed my hand.

"If you had been properly diagnosed sooner," Dr. Mike said, "we could have prevented this much nerve damage from occurring, but there's no turning back the clock on that."

"So what is the cure?" I said.

"The treatment for Hansen's disease is a course of MDT, multi-drug therapy. You'll be on three different medications, starting today. In combination, they work to destroy the bacteria that causes the disease."

"Mycobacterium leprae," I said.

"Precisely." Dr. Mike smiled and glanced at Mom.

"How long will I have to be here?"

"Well, after a few days of taking the medication, you won't be contagious anymore, so you'll be able to go about your normal activities. That's the good news."

"What's the bad news?" Mom said.

"Well, some patients do have severe reactions during treatment, so we ask that you stay for at least four weeks so we can monitor your progress."

I shot Mom a look. An entire month at a leper colony? He had to be kidding. I laughed a little to show him that I had a sense of humor.

Dr. Mike smiled at me and continued. "During that time you will be instructed in foot care and hand care, learn how to prevent injuries, and if anything should arise, we'll be right here to help you through it."

He wasn't kidding.

"And how long will I be on the medication for?"

"Twenty-four months."

"Two years?!"

He nodded.

"I'll be almost twenty!"

"That's still very young, Abby."

"No it isn't!"

He and Mom smiled weakly at each other.

"So, what do I . . . ?"

"You'll be staying down the road at Carville, and you'll be bussed here to the clinic five days a week. Here, you'll work on rehabilitation. Getting strength back into your body. Practicing walking and using your hands and fingers in ways that won't cause further damage. Dangers to look out for. We'll get you fitted for orthotics right away." He glanced down at my feet.

"What about meals?" Mom asked.

"There's a fully staffed kitchen at Carville, so all of your meals will be provided. There are also nursing staff on-site."

"And I'll be living with other . . . other lepers?"

"There are two long-term residents at Carville, plus a number of other out-of-town patients like yourself, staying temporarily. You will have a private room. Like a dorm room." He smiled. Like I was supposed to be excited about that. "There's something else you should know, Abby." He cut his eyes at Mom. "The people here at the clinic, and at Carville where you'll be staying, don't take kindly to that word. And we certainly never use it here at the clinic."

"What word?"

"Leper. Leprosy."

"Huh?" I looked at Mom. She gave me a mini-shrug.

"Some people find it extremely offensive," Dr. Mike said.

"Who does?"

"People who suffer from Hansen's disease."

"You mean leprosy."

"It is now called Hansen's disease, and those afflicted by it are called Hansen's disease sufferers or Hansen's disease patients."

"Lepers."

"No."

"What's the difference what you call it? It's still the most disgusting disease known to humankind!" I put my head in my hands, pressed my fingertips into my eyes. I could call myself whatever I wanted, it didn't change the fact that I was a leper, and in the eyes of my (former) friends and class-mates, I always would be.

"Dr. Rodriguez will talk more about it with you tomorrow," said Dr. Mike, gently.

"Who's that?"

"She's the clinic counselor."

"Oh."

"You'll meet with her once a week as part of your therapy. More often, if you choose."

Mom nodded like this was the best idea she'd heard in ages.

"Do you have any questions?"

"How could I have gotten this?"

Dr. Mike sighed. "Transmission is very difficult to pinpoint. Dr. Rodriguez will talk to you more about how, when and where you might have come into contact with the bacteria."

"Am I going to lose my fingers?"

"Not so long as you're cautious and you take very good care of them."

I nodded, holding back sobs. Mom squeezed my hand again.

"You're going to be okay, Abby," Dr. Mike said. "That's the good news."

"Thank you," Mom said.

He smiled without any teeth and then scribbled some stuff down on a chart. My chart. "I'll see you soon, okay?"

"Okay," I whispered.

Dr. Mike nodded at Mom, then left the room. The door closed behind him with a click.

I stood up and so did my mom. She put her arms around me. She let me tuck my face into the crook of her neck and I let myself be held. She swayed back and forth, rocking me like I was a baby, and I cried like one.

Nobody said much on the drive to Carville. We passed miles of brown fields, barren except for the stubble of sugarcane that had already been harvested. A heaviness hung over us, like I was going to prison or something. Even though I knew I hadn't done anything wrong, I felt guilty. I felt bad. I felt . . . unwanted in the world. I hoped that Dad wouldn't cry when they dropped me off. I could handle Mom crying, but something about seeing your dad cry just makes you crumble inside. I don't know why.

When we arrived at Carville, we had a guided tour of the grounds and inside some of the buildings. We learned that Carville used to be an old sugar plantation. It's a ton of land with a bunch of old colonial buildings on it, settled on the banks of the Mississippi River. It was a leprosarium for over a hundred years. Before 1957, everyone in the United States who was discovered to have leprosy had to go there. Even if they didn't want to. The police would actually arrest them and force them to go. Put them in chains and ship them there in a boxcar. They weren't allowed to phone their families or have visitors or anything. And if they escaped, the police hunted them down and brought them back. They weren't allowed to vote. Just because they had a disease. If a woman with leprosy got pregnant, she wasn't allowed to keep her baby. The doctors back then did all sorts of experiments and research and eventually they actually discovered the cure—sulfone drugs—at Carville.

"Cell phone drugs?" I said.

"Sulfone," said our guide. "With an *s*."

Our guide's name was Irma. She was the head of public relations at Carville and a former patient. But she didn't live there anymore. She lived in Baton Rouge with her husband and her five kids and her dog, Beezley, who sometimes came to work with her.

I half-listened while Irma talked as she showed us around. She didn't look deformed, except for her hand. The fingers were bent at weird angles, like a claw. But she kept it in her pocket most of the time, so I couldn't get a real close look.

Irma told us that in the late 1990s, Carville was a prison for a few years. With real criminals, not just the lepers, and they all lived together. Now, it's the National Hansen's Disease Museum and a cadets camp for at-risk youth, a.k.a., juvenile delinquents, run by the military.

"What kind of, um, supervision will Abby have here?" Dad asked Irma.

"The cadets are supervised twenty-four hours a day if that's what you mean," she said.

Dad nodded.

"And Abby will be able to reach me or the other staff on duty at any time, should the need arise."

Dad nodded again, then smiled at me awkwardly.

Irma led us up the stairs of a two-story red brick building. It looked like an old apartment building. There was a row of white doors, and she opened the first one we came to at the top of the stairs. "This is where you'll be staying while you're with us, Abby," she said, and ushered the three of us inside.

"Wow," Mom said. "It's really nice, hey, Abby?"

Irma beamed.

"Whatever."

Dad cleared his throat and set my luggage down. The suite was nothing to get excited about. It wasn't exactly what I had hoped my first apartment would be like, if you know what I mean. Since it was *in a leper museum*. There was a double bed on an old cast-iron frame, a small wooden table and a dresser, and a hot plate, mini-fridge and toaster oven beside a little sink. There was a tiny bathroom that had only a shower, no tub. The suite smelled like mothballs and Comet.

"There are two other out-of-town patients staying in this building," Irma said. "I'm sure you'll meet them soon."

"Oh, that will be nice for you to have some people to talk to," Mom said.

I glared at her and blinked. She was acting like I was getting dropped off at summer camp, like I was here for *fun*.

"Well," Irma said, "I'll leave you to say your goodbyes. Dinner is served at six-thirty in the mess hall, Abby. You remember how to get there?"

"Yeah. I think so."

"Just give me a shout if you need anything. I'm in the building next door in the front office."

"Okay," I said. "Thanks."

Mom and Dad thanked her and both of them shook her claw-hand, and then she left.

"Well, Abby," Dad said.

"I think it would be easier if you guys left really fast now. Without dragging it out," I said.

"Can we at least give you a hug goodbye?" Mom said.

"You probably shouldn't," I said. "You don't want to get it."

"I already hugged you before anyway," Mom said.

"I know. But you shouldn't have then, either."

"I don't care," she said, coming at me, arms wide. She squished me into her.

Then Dad came and put his arms around the two of us. We stayed like that for a moment, gently swaying back and forth. Dad kissed me on the top of my head. "Love you, kid." He barely ever said that, so it was kind of nice to hear it.

"Me too," I said.

Then the hug broke apart and Mom was wiping her eyes with her sleeve. Dad was all welled up, about to spill over.

"Okay, go on. Get out of here," I said.

Mom opened the door. "Love you, Abby. We'll see you next week for visitor's day."

"Sunday," I said.

She nodded. Then, they were gone.

I sat down on the bed. I had never been that alone before.

The bedspread was white and scratchy. The wooden flooring was old and dinged up. I wondered about all the feet that had walked across that floor. Leprous feet. It gave me the heebie-jeebies to think about it. I wished that I had someone to talk to. I really wanted to text Marla and Liz. But I wouldn't let myself. Not after that kind of betrayal. If people do something like that, they're not your real friends anyway, so good riddance to bad rubbish.

I still missed them like crazy though.

I flopped back on the bed and stared at the ceiling. The ceiling tiles had tiny flecks of gold in them that sparkled when the light hit them just right. I thought about calling Dustin. I was pretty sure I had his number. I looked through the contacts in my phone.

Yep, I had it.

My fingers hovered over the screen. Before I could make up my mind whether to call him or not, there was a knock at the door.

"Um, come in?" I sat up.

A pretty young woman opened the door. Her black hair was in a cute bob and she wore a cream-colored pencil skirt. "Hey," she said, "I'm Jane. I'm staying in the room next door."

"Oh, hi," I said. "I'm Abby."

She moved to cross the floor and shake my hand, but I got weird about it and shoved my hands in my pockets. I don't know why I did that. She had leprosy, so what? *I had it too.*

She stepped back. "I just thought I'd introduce myself." She shrugged. "But if you're busy—"

"No, cool. Yeah. Thanks. I mean, it's nice to meet you."

She sniffed the air. "You want to go for a walk or something? Let this place air out a little?"

I laughed. "Yeah. That's probably a good idea." I opened the windows and we left the room.

Jane was from New York City. She was twenty-seven years old. She'd first been diagnosed when she was eighteen. We walked in the tall grass along the fence line.

"I come here every year for my complete checkup," she said. "And to get a refresher in my physio exercises and stuff. It's been dormant for two years now, but it can come back, so I always make sure to come back to Carville."

"It can come back?" I said. "Like, you mean, after it's cured?"

"Yep. Mine did. It just lies dormant in your cells, but it can rear its ugly head again any old time it wants."

"Just when I thought it couldn't get any worse."

"Mmhm."

"For real, though?"

"Sorry, girl."

"That sucks."

"It's pretty rare for it to happen. I mean, it probably won't happen to you. Want to see the hole in the fence?"

"Um . . . okay?"

"Come on!"

We walked a little farther. A man with a hunched back was mowing the grass about fifty yards away. I wondered if he had leprosy.

"There it is!" Jane pointed to a section of the nine-foot wire fence.

"Um," I said, looking closer. "There's no hole there."

"Yeah, but there's a tunnel *underneath*." She knelt down and swept some dirt away, then lifted up a piece of plywood that had been covered in dirt. "See?"

I peered down into the small, dark hole. It barely seemed big enough for a person to fit through.

"In the early days, when they weren't allowed to leave, someone found this spot where the fence didn't go down as far. They dug underneath it and made a tunnel through to the other side so people could sneak out without getting caught."

"Really?"

"Sure. You could go to Baton Rouge for the night, party, spend the night there even, and come back in the morning. No one would ever know. Obviously it's not the same fence from back then, but they recreated the hole in the same spot as part of the museum."

"Wild."

"Get this," she said. "Are you a romantic?"

"I don't know."

"Well, anyway. The people who met in here and wanted to get married would sneak out through this hole and catch a ride into town to get married."

"Why wouldn't they just get married here? There's a church and everything."

"They weren't allowed! People with leprosy weren't allowed to marry each other!"

"Oh."

"And if they were already married, to someone on the outside, who didn't have leprosy, their husband or wife wasn't allowed to come here and live with them. They could only visit."

"That would suck."

"I know, right?" She ran her fingers along the edge of the hole. Her left ring finger was just a stub, but you could hardly notice because she was so pretty and perfect and put together.

"How do you know all that?"

"Oh, I've read about it," she said. "Plus, two of the old-timers still live here. They have lots of good stories."

"Really?"

"Yeah, Grace and Lester. I'll introduce you later. They've been here for over sixty years, from back when it was mandatory to stay here. Then, when it changed, the government gave them a choice to leave and have their freedom, or stay here and have everything provided, at no cost to them. They chose to stay."

"That's crazy. I would never stay here if I had the choice."

She shrugged. "This is their home."

"It used to be a prison," I said.

"It *used* to be death row," Jane said. "Only the people sentenced to die here didn't commit any crime except getting the disease."

We took a left away from the fence and walked along a gravel path that seemed to have no end.

"Where are we going?" I said.

"Nowhere in particular," Jane said. "Just walking. I thought we'd walk around for a bit and then go to the mess hall. It's not long now till dinnertime. That is, if you want to keep walking . . . ?"

"Yeah, I do," I said.

"I'll show you the lake."

"Okay."

"It's called Lake Johansen. Named after one of the first doctors here."

"You really know a lot about the history here. Are you one of the other guides or something?"

"Nope. Like I said, I've read about it. There's not too much to do around here so there's a lot of time to read. I mean, there's the lake and a golf course and a church, but I don't really peg you as a golfer."

I laughed. "Nope. I've never played."

"Never?"

"Mini-putt."

"Oh, we'll get out there," she said. "It's actually really hard, golf. That's what people don't realize. I mean, it looks pretty relaxed, driving those carts around or walking, getting someone else to carry your bags . . . but, it's actually super difficult."

"My dad plays. It can't be that hard."

Jane laughed.

We rounded a corner and saw about fifty cadets in khaki pants and green shirts doing some kind of drill. We stopped for a moment, watching them.

"*ATTEN*TION!" a guy in camo yelled from the front. They all saluted him.

"Intense," I whispered.

"That's the youth-at-risk program," Jane said.

"Is it all guys?"

"Mostly. I think there are one or two girls." We kept walking.

"So, are they, like, criminals? I mean, young offenders, or . . ."

"Not yet," Jane said.

We walked past them but kept our distance. I stared, I couldn't help it. There was one guy in the front row, he was a mega-babe. He was taller than everyone else and had sandy-brown hair that hung past his ears. We locked eyes. My first thought was, *How can I find him and talk to him?* And my second thought was, *STUPID! Dumbdumbdumbass idiot! He knows why you're here. He knows you're a leper. Why would he even want to be in the same room as you, let alone talk to you? He wouldn't. It would never happen.*

A deep shame burned through me; I wanted to melt into the ground. I wished he'd never seen me. I wished he would have never known. By this point, I was staring at the ground, but I took one last glance at him, and he was *still* looking at me. Damn. Jane cut her eyes at me.

"You like a man in uniform?"

"I'm not totally opposed to a man in uniform," I said.

She laughed. "So you're in school still?" She steered me left at a fork in the path.

"Yep."

"What grade?"

"Twelfth."

"Ahh, a senior."

"Mmhm."

"You like high school?"

"Yeah, I mean, I did. I used to like it, before I got sick."

Jane nodded. "You were popular, right?"

"I guess, yeah."

"That's hard," she said. "You know what no one ever tells you about high school?"

"What?"

"That it repeats over and over again, throughout your whole life." She tucked her hair behind her ears.

"What? What are you talking about?"

"I'm saying that being an adult is the same as being in high school, except with money. Life is perpetual high school."

"No," I said.

She nodded. "It's true."

"I don't believe you."

"You'll see."

"But—"

"Let me guess, you were one of the most popular girls in school, one of the most beautiful, all the guys wanted to go out with you, etcetera, etcetera."

"Not exactly," I said.

"But pretty close, right?"

I shrugged. "I don't know."

"Well, listen. Girls who get by on looks and luck alone get a real shock once they get older. Their looks don't get them what they want all the time anymore. It's the brainy girls who get the best jobs and the great husbands, because those girls are relying on something that lasts, something of real value. So now, in your senior year, you get Hansen's disease. Not the worst thing in the world. Not the worst timing either. Because *now* you can start working on other aspects of yourself," Jane said. "Not just focusing on your appearance all the time."

"What makes you think you know so much about me?"

"Look at me," she said. "Do you think I'm so different from you? I was exactly where you are now, ten years ago."

We walked in silence for a while. Songbirds chirped in a tree above us. I kicked at a rock in the path. I looked at Jane out of the corner of my eye. She looked like someone who told the truth. I didn't know whether or not to be offended by what she'd said. But as far as I could tell, she was my best chance at social interaction, and I didn't want to buck it up and be a loner for the next four weeks.

"Someone should make a movie like that," I said. "Where the characters repeat high school until they're old. Sort of like *Groundhog Day*, except the characters actually age."

"That could be funny," Jane said. "I'd watch it, for sure."

"What's your job?" I said. "I mean . . . do you have a job?"

"Yeah." She laughed. "I'm a waitress at Junior's."

"What's Junior's?"

"Sorry. Junior's Most Fabulous Cheesecakes and Desserts. It's in Brooklyn."

"I like cheesecake."

"Most people do. Hey, you should come in next time you're in New York. I'll give you a slice on the house."

I laughed. "I've never been to New York."

"Oh, honey."

"I was planning to go to L.A. for university, but I don't know if that's going to happen now. I mean . . . because of . . ."

"Well, I always say there are two kinds of people," Jane said.

"Yeah?"

"L.A. people and New York people."

"What about Austin people?"

"Honey, nobody gives a rat's pitoot about Austin people."

I laughed. "You're probably right."

"There's the lake." She pointed to a small man-made lake in the middle of the field. Some ducks floated on the surface and willow trees leaned over the edge, dipping their branches in the water.

"Nice," I said.

"There's a little rowboat you can take out on it if you want."

"Yeah?"

"Might have a hole in it though. I'm not sure."

"Huh," I said. "Seems . . . risky."

"Hey, they gotta keep it interesting around here somehow, right?" Jane maneuvered us toward a huge white building. "Ready for dinner?"

"Is it edible?"

"Most of the time." She put her arm around my shoulders. "Come on."

The dining hall was full of cadets when we walked in. There were over a hundred of them in there. They made a terrible racket that bounced off the high ceilings. Jane led me down the aisle between the rows of long tables. In the corner closest to the kitchen was a table that had a sign that said RESERVED on it. Jane walked to the other side of the table, taking long elegant strides. She pulled out a chair.

"Um," I said. "Are you sure we can sit here? It says reserved."

She sat down. "Abby. Who do you think it's reserved for?"

"Oh. Right." I took a seat, feeling sheepish.

Most of the cadets were already eating, but some were still in line, waiting for their food. *He* was in line. Tall guy. From before. On the field. We locked eyes for the second time that day. He grinned at me. I turned away, scratching my neck.

"Sorry, what?" I snuck another peek at him.

"I didn't say anything," Jane said. She followed my line of sight. "Oh no. Don't even."

"What?"

"Never mind. I don't want to know. I mean, I *do* want to know, but not right now. It'll spoil my appetite."

I looked at her and she made a goofy face. I couldn't help laughing.

"Oh look, here come Grace and Lester," Jane said. "You'll love them. They're so sweet."

I turned around. An ancient gray-haired couple ambled into the dining hall. They both wore huge sunglasses. The man had a white cane that he whacked around and the woman clung to his arm, her humped back rising almost above her head. "Jeez," I said. "Talk about the blind leading the blind."

Jane turned to me, sharp. "Yeah, they're blind. They got Hansen's disease before there were sulfone drugs. The bacteria attacked the nerves in their eyes. *You'd* be going blind too in the next few years if it weren't for the drugs."

"Sorry. I'm sorry. I don't know why I said that."

"It's okay," Jane said. "You're just young . . . and stupid." Her mouth twitched into a half-smirk.

"It's true that I'm young," I said.

She rolled her eyes. "Come on, let's get in line."

When we lined up, the three cadets ahead of us skooched in closer to put distance between us and them. They eyed us up and down and whispered to each other. It hurt, but somehow having Jane there with me made it hurt less.

"If they're scared of getting close to us, I'd hate to see what they're going to be like in Afghanistan," she said.

"I guess they'll still piss their pants," I said. "Just more frequently."

"More fervently," Jane said.

"So will all of them be in the military eventually?" I said.

"Not all, I don't think. But a lot of them, if they're not in jail," Jane said, shrugging.

A boy ahead of us laughed and his buddy stuck out his tongue as if he were gagging on it.

"What do you have to do to land in here anyway?" I said.

"Basically you have to be more of an asshole than the people around you deem necessary. From what I've ascertained, these guys are the cream of the crop."

My cadet was about ten people ahead of us. I could see the back of his head, towering above everyone else's.

He had a pale scar on the back of his neck in the shape of a crescent moon. I wondered how he got it. I wanted to trace my finger over it.

"Grace! Lester!" Jane called. She waved, senselessly. "I'm saving you a spot in line."

They both smiled and made their way toward us. As they got closer, I could see that Grace's nose had been re-sculpted before advances in plastic surgery. It looked like someone had stuck a small pinecone where her nose used to be. The nostrils were all wrong too. She was brittle and mangled. It was hard to look at her. I shivered. Both Lester's and Grace's hands were gnarled and crab-like, but it was hard to tell if that was from the disease or old age or arthritis or what. They looked to be about a hundred years old.

"Grace, Lester, I want you to meet Abby. She's a temporary resident. Abby, this is Grace."

"Hello." Grace extended her hand, nearly hitting me in the boob.

I grabbed her hand and shook it gently; it was as dry and papery as an onion-skin.

"And this is Lester," Jane said.

"Tabby?" Lester thrust his strange hand toward me.

"Abby," I said.

"Gabby?"

"ABBY!" Jane yelled in his ear.

"Oh, I'm sorry." He tapped his hearing aid. "Battery's going on me again," he said. "Abby, it's a real pleasure to meet you."

"Thank you," I said. "It's nice to meet you too."

"Where are you from, Abby?" Grace asked.

"Texas," I said.

"Oh! We just love Texans. Are you a rancher?" Lester asked.

"No," I said, giggling. "I'm a cheerleader. Well, I was, before . . ."

"No kidding," Jane said, rolling her eyes.

"Oh, my. How wonderful," Grace said.

"Can you do backflips and everything?" Jane said.

"Well, I can't do *everything*, but I can do backflips, yeah."

"Do one," Jane said.

"Right now?"

"Right here. Right now. Show us."

Lester nodded and Grace clapped her hands together.

"I . . . I can't."

"Why not?"

"I'm not warmed up."

"Aw, come on," Jane said. "Just one. One measly back-flip. I'll let you have my dessert . . ."

"Oh yes, come on, please," Lester said.

"But you can't even see it," I said.

"But I'll know," he said. "I'll *know* you did it."

"Come on!" Jane said.

I looked up at the ceiling and took a deep breath. "Fine." I pulled my phone out of my pocket. "Hold this." I handed it to Jane.

"Yay!"

Grace squealed, clenching Lester's arm.

There was a wide space around me with no tables and no cadets. I took a little run down the aisle and did a front flip (to warm up) and then a standing backflip. Then I raised both arms in a finishing stance, just like I would have at a real game.

The entire dining hall exploded into applause, people whistled and cheered. I took a little curtsy, scanning the crowd for my cadet. He was watching from a nearby table, a lopsided smile on his face. A warm glow swelled up in me. I made my way back to Jane. She slapped me on the back, giddy with laughter. "I didn't think you'd actually do it," she said, chuckling.

"That was really something," Grace said.

"But you—"

"I could *feel* it," she said. "In here." She placed her gnarled hand over her heart.

After dinner, Jane and I walked Grace and Lester back to their cottage. They were all still laughing and going on about my backflip. Jane said I should audition for Cirque du Soleil.

"Yeah. Right. Because I want to spend my whole life surrounded by freaks," I said. "That's my idea of a good time."

They all looked away. Well, Lester was kind of half-looking at me, but he wasn't seeing me, obviously. I thought about saying sorry to them, but then that would be like admitting that I was calling them freaks. So I said nothing. Lester began to whistle a sad little tune. We walked on as the light faded, the pecan trees casting long shadows over the grass.

"Well, this is our stop," Lester said as his cane slapped against the wooden gate in front of their place. Jane and I said good night to them and went back to our apartment building.

"Want to come in for a tea or something?" Jane asked.

I yawned. "I'm actually pretty tired. I might just crash."

She nodded. "You've had a big day."

"Yeah."

"Okay, well, get some rest. I'll see you in the morning."

"What time does the bus take us to the clinic again?"

"Nine a.m. sharp."

"Early."

"Breakfast is at seven-thirty."

"Ugh. I might just grab something to go."

"Well, I always say there are two kinds of people," Jane said.

"Yeah, you said—"

"Morning people and night people."

"Oh."

"I guess we know which category you're in."

"What about afternoon people?"

"Afternoon people don't stand a chance."

"Huh?"

"Think about it," Jane said. "Everything of consequence happens either in the morning or at night. Nothing important ever happens in the afternoon. People take naps in the afternoon."

"The afternoon is Austin," I said.

"Exactly."

"Okay, well, I guess I'll see you in the morning," I said.

"Good night, hon."

"Night, Jane."

Even though I was super tired, I didn't think I'd be able to sleep. The bed was like a cement platform and the blanket was like a burlap sack. I tossed and turned for what felt like hours. I couldn't get comfortable. I realized that I might never be comfortable again. There are those Buddhist sayings, "All life is pain. Life is suffering." I'd never paid much attention to them before. But what if they were actually right? People say life is short. But what if they're wrong? What if the truth is, life is really, really long? Excruciatingly long. Then what?

When I stepped out of my apartment the next morning, I was met by a yellow wall of fur. This scrawny yellow Lab swarmed my legs, jumping up to lick my face and barking in a friendly, needy way.

"Hey, buddy," I said, kneeling down to pet him. He went crazy, panting and pawing my thighs and trying to lick my face. I laughed, pushing his head away.

"I'm sorry! I'm so sorry!" Irma ran out of her office, waving her arms, yelling. "Beezley, get down here! You git! You no-good, filthy animal!"

"It's okay," I called to her. Beezley nuzzled my neck. "It's actually kind of nice," I said quietly. I petted Beezley some more and then stood up and started to climb down the steps. Beezley followed me every step of the way until we were down on the ground, and then Irma grabbed his collar.

"I'm so sorry. I don't know what's gotten into him. He isn't usually like this."

"It's alright," I said.

She scolded him and he wagged his tail, panting and grinning.

"Did you sleep okay?" Irma asked.

"Yeah," I lied. "Pretty good."

"Anything you need?"

A new face. A new body, I thought. *A dog who will love me when humans no longer can.* "No," I said. "I'm okay."

"Okay, well, just let us know if you think of anything," Irma said.

"Thanks," I said. "Will do."

Beezley's tail slapped against her leg as she dragged him back toward her office.

I gazed after them for a moment, then made my way toward the mess hall for breakfast.

M y first day of therapy at the clinic went pretty much as you'd expect. I got fitted for orthotics and was told by Charlotte, the physiotherapist, that I should wear them all the time inside the special support shoes they gave me. The shoes were brown and shaped like livers and literally the ugliest footwear in existence.

"So, you're saying I have to wear these *all* the time?"

"All the time."

"What about at the beach?"

"Definitely at the beach."

"What about when I want to wear heels?"

"You shouldn't ever be wearing heels, Abby."

"But . . . I'm . . . I have to."

"Why do you have to?"

"Because. I'm seventeen."

"Look. This is what happens to people with nerve damage in their feet and ankles like you have. They step off a curb the wrong way and break their ankle, but because there's no sensation, they don't *feel* it. They don't know they're injured. And so they keep walking on the joint, doing more and more damage to it. In some cases, it gets so bad that the foot needs to be amputated."

"Ugh!"

"That's right. See, that's what most people don't realize about the effects of Hansen's disease. It's not the disease *itself* that causes people to lose digits and limbs, it's the absence of sensation that's the most dangerous."

"Pain," I said.

"Yes! Pain! Pain is a great gift. Healthy bodies experience pain. Pain keeps us safe."

"I have pain."

"I know you do, Abby," she said gently.

"Just not in my feet and hands."

She nodded. "That's why you have to be so careful to protect them and keep them out of harm's way. These shoes are one way of doing that."

I knew I would still wear my flip-flops at the beach. I knew I would still wear heels to dress up. But I just nodded and said okay because I knew that Charlotte was trying to help me, and that's what she wanted to hear. We talked about ways to protect my hands and fingers. Like don't stick them into boiling water (duh!); be extra-vigilant when using scissors, knives, and sharp tools; wear mittens and gloves in the fall, winter, and early spring, even if you don't think it's cold, even if you think you don't need to. Frostbite is the number one reason people with the disease lose fingers.

She gave me a stress ball with a yellow happy face on it and had me squeeze it twenty-five times with each hand. I was supposed to do that four times a day. Then Charlotte wrapped both my feet and hands in hot, white towels and gave them all a little massage. It was no Pink Orchid Day Spa, but it felt pretty nice.

"Thanks," I said when she was finished.

"You're welcome. I'll just let you rest here for a few minutes."

"Okay," I said.

She dimmed the lights as she left the room and I dozed off. I don't know how long I was out for. The next thing I knew, a short, round woman was knocking on the wall beside my head.

"What? Oh. Sorry. I—"

"Abby?"

"Yes?"

"I'm Dr. Gabriella Rodriguez." She extended her hand and I unwrapped the towel from mine and we shook. Her nails were painted green and she wore chunky silver and turquoise rings on each of her fingers.

"Hi," I said.

"I'll be your counselor while you're here."

"Okay."

"Would you like to step into my office?" It was one of those questions that's not really a question at all. Adults are always pulling stunts like that. Pretending you have a choice when you actually don't. Giving you a false sense of power so you're not crushed by the reality of your situation.

"Uh, sure," I said. I unwrapped the rest of the towels and followed her down the narrow hallway into a tiny office. It seemed more like a storage closet than an office. There were no windows. Just a bunch of those cheesy motivational posters that all the school counselors have. A poster of a guy climbing a mountain that said, "Go for the Summit!" A poster of a runner breaking through a finish-line ribbon that said, "Success Is Never Giving Up!" I thought these posters were cruel and totally inappropriate for Dr. Rodriguez to have in her office, considering that people with leprosy would probably never run a marathon or climb a mountain or do any of the other junk in the pictures, like fly in a rocket ship ("Reach for the Stars!") or become a professional figure skater ("Live Your Dreams!"). I positioned myself in the chair so I wouldn't have to look at them.

"Would you like a glass of water or anything?" she asked.

"A double shot of your best bourbon."

She raised an eyebrow, unimpressed.

"Hehe. Just kidding," I said.

"Umhm."

I crossed and uncrossed my legs.

"So, Abby," Dr. Rodriguez said. "How are you feeling?"

"How am I feeling? Really?"

She spread her arms as if to say, *bring it on.*

"I'm a teenage leper. I mean, does it get any worse than that?"

"Hansen's disease patient," she corrected.

"You know, I really don't see what difference it makes *what* you call it. Changing the name of it doesn't make it any easier. It doesn't make it go away."

Dr. Rodriguez sighed. "The word *leper* has a long, awful history, Abby. Think about that word; it's a noun."

What was this, English class?

"Yeah . . . ?"

"So it objectifies people. It labels them *as* their disease instead of a person suffering *from* a disease. They become identified as nothing more than the disease. Think about it. We don't call people who have chicken pox 'chicken

149

poxers.' We don't call people living with HIV 'HIVers.' They're people first. The word *leper* robs Hansen's disease sufferers of their identity. Someone might be a mother, a wife, a knitter, a golfer, an astronaut, a dog-lover, but if we call her a leper, we reduce her to just that one thing."

"Exactly," I said. "It takes over. It trumps all the other things."

"Not necessarily."

"You know what? *I* have the disease, okay. You don't. I think that gives me the right to call it whatever I want. If I want to call myself a leper, that's my business."

"Fine." She folded her hands together. "But please know that the L-word is not used here in the clinic or at Carville. And if you do use it, people will be deeply, deeply offended and hurt."

"Okay. I get it."

"Alright. So, Abby." She reached for a pen and piece of paper and slid them across her desk to me. "I'd like you to make me a list."

"Uh. What kind of list?"

"A list of all the emotions you've experienced since you were first diagnosed with Hansen's disease."

"Oh boy."

She slid across the entire stack of paper. "Use as much as you want," she said. "I'm just going to refill my coffee, and I'll be back in a few minutes. Don't worry if you're not finished by then. Take as much time as you need."

"Okay," I said.

"Good." She moved toward the door.

"Dr. Rodriguez?"

"Yes, Abby?"

"Would you bring me a coffee too, please?"

"How do you take it?"

"Lots of cream, lots of sugar."

"You got it."

Then she was gone, and I was left staring at the blank sheet of paper in front of me.

I sat for a minute, not writing anything. I reached across the desk and took a red Sharpie out of Dr. Rodriguez's pencil cup. I clicked the lid on and off for a while. Then I started writing.

This is what my list looked like:

My Emotions after Diagnosis

- shock
- anger
- RAGE
- why me?
- ~~unfairness~~ injustice
- SCARED!
- fear
- hate everyone

- grief
- depression
- helplessness
- mad
- UNCLEAN!
- wanting to die
- HORROR
- sadness

- GROSS
- hopeless
- failure at life
- rejected
- heartbroken
- WHY???!!!
- afraid
- disgust

When Dr. Rodriguez returned, I was staring at the poster of the rocket ship, wishing I was on it, going to another planet, living a different life, any other life but mine. I wouldn't even mind having another disease. Gonorrhea, maybe. Or some form of non-fatal cancer, even. Just not leprosy. Anything but leprosy.

She placed my coffee in front of me.

"Thanks," I said. Steam rose from the mug. The mug had a rainbow on it and said "Where there's rain, there are rainbows." I wanted to throw it against the wall and see it shatter into Skittles.

"May I?" Dr. Rodriguez reached for my list.

I nodded.

She peeled it off the desk and sat down heavily in her chair. I watched her face as she read through it. She was half-smiling, which I didn't think was very respectful since none of it was funny. She placed the sheet of paper between us and looked up at me. "I want to tell you that all of these emotions are completely normal and valid."

"Okay."

"Would you like to talk about any of them?"

"Not really."

"What would you like to talk about?"

"I don't know."

"Anything at all. Doesn't have to relate to Hansen's disease."

"Why did this happen to me?" I burst out crying.

I guess making a list of intense emotions somehow unlocks them. Tricky, Rodriguez. Real tricky.

She pushed a box of Kleenex across the desk and I grabbed a handful. I wiped my face and blew my nose. Dr. Rodriguez cleared her throat. "Have you ever come into contact with a nine-banded armadillo?"

"What? That's a joke, right?"

"I'm afraid not."

She explained that about a third of new cases of Hansen's disease in the United States, the cases where people hadn't contracted it from somewhere abroad, occur in Texas, Florida and Louisiana. They think because those states have a high population of armadillos. And, like I told you before, armadillos can transmit the disease to humans (and vice versa).

I sifted through all of my memories. I'd seen them dead on the side of the road lots of times, but I couldn't remember ever touching one. I knew kids at school made fun of people who ate them. Rednecks ate them. Had *I* ever eaten armadillo meat?

My heart seized, remembering the church barbecue. "Oh, *God!*"

Dr. Rodriguez nodded slowly.

"I might have eaten one. But that was ages ago! I was only nine or ten."

She nodded. "Hansen's disease has a very long incubation period. Typically, five to twenty years."

I stared at her. She blinked, meeting my gaze. This was all real and no one was joking. That was the unbelievable part.

"FML," I said.

"Pardon me?"

"I want to see a lawyer," I said.

"Why is that?"

"I want to sue the church for damages."

"That's an understandable response, Abby. However, I have to say, there would be no way to prove that you did indeed contract the disease that day."

"It had to be that day. I've had no other contact with an armadillo. I've never met another person with lep—, uh, Hansen's disease."

"You could have met someone with an active case and not have known it."

"But—"

"Abby. The important thing now is for you to focus on your rehabilitation and recovery."

"But—"

"While it's a perfectly legitimate response for you to be angry and want to seek retribution, I don't think getting involved in a legal battle against the church is going to do us any good at this point."

"Us?" Why was she saying *us*? It was *me* who had leprosy. Not us.

"I'm part of your recovery team, Abby. Everyone on staff here is. You're not alone in this, okay?"

"Whatever."

She sighed. "You're not going to believe me right now, and I don't blame you, but you are going to be alright. You're going to survive this and you're going to be stronger for it."

"Yeah? Well, what if I don't *want* to be stronger? What if I want to go back to being a little weakling? A little weakling who didn't have *leprosy*."

"Unfortunately, that's not really an option, is it?"

"No mulligans," I mumbled.

Dr. Rodriguez brightened. "Are you a golfer? There's a beautiful course at Carville."

I folded my arms and put my head down on her desk and cried. Fucking armadillos.

At dinner I sat at the reserved table again with Jane, Grace, Lester and the other temporary resident, Barry, who was a fat, balding man with orange plastic glasses that made his eyes look like enormous beetles. He was one of those men who could be twenty-five or forty-five, but it was difficult to tell. Life hadn't been easy on him, that much was clear. I mean, obviously. He was here. He kept his hands in his pockets most of the time, but I saw them when he ate, and they were mitten-hands: normal thumbs with stubby fingers. Lester tried to engage him in conversation, but he only grunted and shoveled forkfuls of food into his mouth. You'd think he had gone weeks without eating, the way he pounded it. It was spaghetti Bolognese and watching the red sauce dribble down Barry's double chin was making me lose my appetite. Sure, he couldn't help having leprosy, I could forgive him that, but couldn't he at least have table manners? His BO wafted across the table. I put my head down and wished to be anywhere but here.

Jane elbowed me in the ribs and I looked up. My cadet was walking by. He looked right at me and smiled. I smiled back and he smiled bigger. Maybe there was some of the old me left after all. The girl who could turn heads, the girl who could capably flirt, before she turned into a social pariah, a horror show.

Then his buddies at another table called to him. That's how I learned his name: Scott. He nodded to his friends and went to join them. Jane whistled low through her teeth. "Somebody's got it bad," she said.

I didn't say anything. I concentrated on trying not to blush.

"You have to find a way to talk to him," Jane said.

"No." I shook my head.

"Yes." She nodded.

"Why would he want to talk to me? I mean, bad acne is one thing, but *this*?" I pointed to my puffy, bumpy pizza face. "This is on a whole new level."

"Yeah, but maybe he *also* knows that you're going to

recover and that you're probably not contagious anymore. Maybe he's forward thinking."

"I thought I was still contagious for another week," I said.

"You're missing my point."

"What *is* your point?"

"My point is that you have to talk to that hottie!" She slapped my arm playfully.

"There's no point." I turned back to my spaghetti. "He's probably just taking the piss."

"Huh?"

"You know, making fun. *Pretending* to flirt with me to make his friends laugh. Besides, he's a criminal. Isn't that the reason these guys are here? To keep them out of juvie?"

"You've got too many excuses, girl."

"Those aren't excuses. Those are legitimate reasons."

Jane raised a meticulously tweezed eyebrow at me.

"Jane. Look. It'll never happen. You don't meet someone you're going to be in a relationship with at a lep—" I coughed. "At a place like this."

Lester cleared his throat.

"Where do you think Grace and Lester met?" Jane said.

I looked at the old blind couple, snuggled up beside each other slurping their spaghetti, two peas in a pod. "That's different," I said.

"Why?"

I lowered my voice. "Because they both have it."

Jane eyed my cadet. "He's got some kind of problems," she said with a shrug. "Else he wouldn't be here, doing baby-army camp."

I watched Scott from across the room. He tilted his head back and let out a big belly laugh at something another guy had said. I could tell by the way he laughed that he wasn't an evil person. Was it possible that his smiles for me were genuine? That he wasn't just doing it to be cruel? What guy in his right mind would want to date a leper? It was wholly ridiculous. And yet . . . There it was again. That glance. That grin. Dammit.

"What have you got to lose?" Jane said.

She was right. From where I was, there was no place left to go but up.

After dessert, Jane and I left together. I stalled as we were leaving the mess hall, pretending to tie my liver-shoe, so that I'd be going through the doors at the same time as Scott. I accidentally on-purpose brushed up against his arm as we passed each other. He didn't jerk away like I'd expected him to. He turned to me.

"Hi," I said.

"Hi," he said, grinning.

"Hi." I froze. "Ugh, I'm sorry. I hadn't planned what to say to you beyond that." *Idiot.*

He laughed. "I'm Scott." He held out his hand. There was no hesitation. No flinching. No pulling it back and sliding it through his hair, saying, *Psych!* He knew that I had this terrible disease and he was going to shake my hand anyway. I took his hand. It was big and warm and strong.

"Abby," I said.

"Great to meet you, Abby."

I liked the way my name sounded in his mouth. I wished he would say it again.

"Dude! Let's go!" His friend shoved him from behind and he was swept away from me in a sea of green and khaki.

His friends were razzing him, to be sure. I could almost hear them saying, *Dude, that's gross. You're gonna get it from her! Are you stupid or something? What were you thinking?* But he looked back at me and smiled, and I knew that whatever they were saying didn't matter to Scott.

And not to me, either.

The rest of the week was more of the same, but I didn't have to meet with Dr. Rodriguez again, and I was glad for it. The medication seemed to be working because the spots on my face were fading and my eyes and cheeks had lost nearly all of their puffiness. The other spots on my body were starting to fade as well and the scaly patches were flaking away to smooth skin underneath. I still felt tired and weak, but I was trying to "focus on the positives" like Dr. Rodriguez advised.

When I saw Scott at meal times, he would say hi and I would say hi back if we happened to be close enough to hear each other. Then I'd get giddy for a minute or two, and then I'd beat myself up for even entertaining the idea that he might ever in a billion years be interested in me. But then I'd sneak a look at him across the dining hall and he'd be looking at me, and I'd have to work to beat down the butterflies in my stomach. Jane would tease me and I'd tell her to shut up, and that's pretty much how it went for the first week. Then, Friday night after jambalaya soup, he came over to the reserved table as I was finishing my last bite.

"Hey, Abby," he said, towering over us.

"Oh. Hi, Scott."

Grace and Lester looked in his general direction. Barry fidgeted with his fork and knife, and Jane stared up at Scott like he was some kind of Greek god, which, let's face it, he kind of was.

"I was wondering if you'd like to go for a walk with me? We get some free time after dinner tonight, so . . . That is, if you're free. I mean, if you're not busy. Or, are you done eating? I'm sorry, you're not done yet, are you?"

Lester had his tongue jammed into the side of his cheek and Grace nodded, slow and sure. Jane kicked me under the table.

"Yeah. Yes. I'm done." I stood up.

Lester cackled, not in an unfriendly way.

"Are you sure?" Scott said.

"Positive. Let's go." I was in such a hurry to go with him, that I left my dishes on the table instead of putting them away in their proper bins like we were supposed to.

"Cool," he said.

"You kids have fun now!" Jane called after us. I could hear Grace giggling as we walked out of the mess hall.

"Where would you like to go?" Scott said.

"Oh, I don't care. Doesn't matter."

"You're right," he said. "Let's just walk along the river for a while."

"Great," I said.

Neither of us talked for a minute, then we both started to say something at the same time. We laughed.

"You go ahead," he said.

"I was just going to ask you where you're from," I said.

"Oklahoma."

"Wow, a real live Okie."

"Born and bred. How about you?"

"Texas," I said.

"I figured."

"How'd you figure?"

"All the prettiest girls are from Texas."

I laughed. "And they know when they're being fed a line."

He turned away from me toward the river. It looked black and bottomless in the fading light. "Sorry," he said, smiling. "That one usually works."

Neither of us said anything for a while. The river rushed and burbled beside us, filling the night air with its hurried noises.

"So, you're sick, huh?" Scott said.

"Nope. Thought I'd just hang out here for a while. Kind of a mini-vacay sort of thing . . ."

He raised his eyebrow.

"Why are you here?" I asked.

"Same thing," he said. "Needed a little R&R, thought, why not try a boot camp? Those are relaxing, right?"

We laughed. An owl swooped over us and we watched it soar over the gnarled oak trees.

"Seriously, though," Scott said. "That has to be rough."

"Yep." I nodded. "I actually can't imagine how it could possibly be any worse."

"Well, you could have not met me . . . That would be way worse."

"Better get a rod and reel for all those lines you're casting, Scott."

He laughed.

"Now you," I said.

"Me, what?"

"You tell me why you're at a camp for juvenile delinquents."

"I'm a bad man, Abby," he said, grinning. "A very bad man."

"Uh-huh."

"The baddest. You should stay away from me, actually."

"Oh yeah?"

"Yeah."

"What did you do?"

"What haven't I done?"

"Are you going to tell me or what?"

"Or what."

"So, that's a no?"

He scratched his chin. "That's a not now, maybe later."

"Okay," I said.

"Okay?"

"Okay."

"Cool."

"Can I ask you something?" I said.

"Shoot."

"Why did you talk to me?"

"Why not?" He shrugged.

"But, you know I'm sick. Doesn't that freak you out?"

"No. Should it?"

"I don't know. Probably."

"I read about it online. It's not that bad as long as you get treatment. And you started taking the pills already, right?"

"Yeah, last Sunday."

"Yeah, so you're not even contagious anymore."

"But how can you be so cool about it? I mean, even my best friends weren't . . . Okay, let's just say, they were very un-cool about it. But you don't even know me and—"

"Look, I wanted to talk to you, so I talked to you. What's the big deal?"

"Yeah, but *why*?"

"Okay. You want to know the truth?"

"*Yes!*"

"It was your backflip."

"My backflip?" I laughed.

"Yeah. I saw you do that flip and I thought, wow. I have to talk to that girl." He shrugged. "That was it."

"Huh. That's . . ."

"Look, let's just say I know how it feels to be treated like an outcast, okay? No one deserves that. Especially not a beautiful blonde gymnast."

"Cheerleader."

"Sorry. Beautiful blonde cheerleader."

"I *was* a cheerleader. Not anymore, I guess."

"Why not anymore?"

"Lost all my strength. Plus, I'm here for at least another three weeks, so I'll be missing most of the spring season anyway. Pretty much guarantees I'm off the team."

"That sucks."

"It's pretty much ruined my life," I said.

"Wow. You're really serious about cheerleading." He laughed a little bit.

I told him about how it meant missing out on the USC scholarship. How I wouldn't be able to afford university now or be able to study acting in California like I had been planning for longer than I can remember.

"Abby! You can't let this slip through your fingers! There must be something you can do!"

"Scott. Calm down."

"But—"

"It's okay. It's not going to happen. It's my own stupid fault. I put all my eggs in one basket."

"The cheerleading basket."

I nodded. "Sometimes, your eggs get broken."

"But . . . but, this is serious! This was your lifelong *dream*!"

"Lots of people have dreams," I said. "Doesn't mean everyone gets to live them."

"I think you still have to try. Maybe your coach will make an exception or something. Say that you were part of the team anyway."

"I doubt it."

"You could ask though," he said.

"You're right. I could ask."

There was a cool wind and I shivered as I wrapped my arms around myself.

"You cold?" Scott said.

"I'm okay."

"Here." He took off his sweater and placed it over my shoulders.

"Thanks."

"So, you'll ask, right? I mean, it's the least you can do."

"Okay, yeah. You're right. I'll ask her."

"Good." He grinned. "Then, when you get your first movie, you can make sure to thank me in the credits."

"Alright." I laughed.

He was kind of weird, but I liked him. Plus he was hot, so that always helps. He talked a little bit about his mom and dad (divorced); his older brother, Jesse (still living in his mom's basement); and his golden retriever, Tinker Bell.

"Tinker Bell?"

"Tink for short," he said.

"Did you name her?"

"Yeah! Don't you think it's a pretty name?"

I giggled.

"It's one of my favorite girl's names. If I ever have a daughter, I might name her Tinker Bell. Do you like it?"

I looked at him.

"I mean, I'm not asking you because of that or anything. Oh no. No. Don't think that! I'm just asking you if you like the name."

"I think I like it more for a dog than for a person," I said.

"That's fair, I guess."

We walked along the riverside without saying anything for a few minutes. The early stars glinted above us. I pulled the sleeves of Scott's sweater down over my hands. His sweater was gray and soft and smelled like a pumpkin spice latte. I looked up at him. He wore a half-smile and looked peaceful. How could he have done something bad enough to get sent here? He was so cute. He was so nice.

"Should we go back now?" he said. "Can I walk you home?"

"Sure. Okay."

"But not home, home, to Texas. Just to the building you're staying in here."

"Right."

We turned around and headed toward my apartment.

"You have your own room?" he said.

"Yeah. It's a whole suite, actually."

"Whoa. Lucky. I have to share with, like, twenty other guys."

"Bunk beds?"

"Military issue."

"Yuck."

He nodded. "Total yuck."

"When do you get to go home?" I said.

"Well, my mom said she's done with me. So I guess, never?"

"So I guess I'll see you tomorrow then," I said.

"And the day after that."

"Okay." I grinned back at him.

"Can I have a hug good night?"

"Are you sure you want to? You're not afraid of—"

"Oh, shut up already with that." He put his arms around me. I hesitated, then patted his back awkwardly. He was warm and I could feel his muscles through his shirt. My forehead rested against his sternum as he held me. It was nice. Really nice. If I let myself, I could imagine being his girlfriend. I could imagine falling in love with him. The engagement party. The beach wedding. The kids and the dog and the hammock in the yard, swinging gently in the breeze. I could imagine all of it. But I wouldn't let myself. I counted my breaths instead. Finally, he let go. "Good night, Abby."

"Good night, Scott." I began to climb the stairs up to my suite, forgetting everything I'd learned that week about foot placement and proper alignment and stability while doing stairs. But I made it anyway. I waved to Scott as I unlocked the door to my room. And he waved back.

I was in my room only a few seconds when there was a tap on the door.

"Who is it?"

Jane poked her head in.

"Oh. Hi," I said.

"*Heyyy.*"

I rolled my eyes. "Come in."

She grabbed my hand and twirled me around. "Are you going to have his babies?"

"No! Stop!" I said, laughing.

"Oooh! He gave you his sweater!"

"Oh, shoot. I forgot to give it back." I took it off and hung it on the back of the door.

"For-got." Jane made air quotes with her fingers.

"I did!"

"Soon you'll forget to take your tongue out of his mouth too. Or did you do that already?"

"No! Jane, please. Stop, okay? It's not like that."

"Umhm." She nodded. "Just remember, honey. No glove, no love."

"Aargh. Enough." I pushed her toward the door. "I'll see you tomorrow, okay?"

"What?! You're kicking me out? You're not going to tell me about your date?"

"It wasn't a date. And . . . yes."

"Fine," she said. "I was just leaving anyways."

"Okay."

"Okay. Good. Then."

"Good *night*, Jane."

She made a kissy-face at me, crossing her eyes.

"Jane!"

She turned around and did that thing with your hands rubbing up and down your body where it looks like you're making out with someone.

"Bye," I said, shoving her out of my room. I shut the door behind her and locked it. I could hear her laughing through the window and couldn't help but smile. I sat on my bed and held my palms to my cheeks. I could tell I was blushing without even having to look in the mirror. I had an overwhelming impulse to text Marla and Liz. But I didn't. I kicked off my shoes and flopped back on my bed and stared at the ceiling and wondered about all the people before me who had done the same thing in this very room. What had happened to them? What would happen to me?

The next morning, Jane and I had breakfast together. Lester and Grace liked to sleep late, apparently, and no one knew where Barry was. Jane was making googly-eyes and kissy-lips at me.

"The thing is, I don't get it," I said.

"Don't get what?"

"Why would he hit on me? Why would he flirt with me? I'm not pretty right now. Look at me, I look like a strawberry pie that a horse stepped on. I'm gross."

Jane rolled her eyes. "It's not that bad. Your face has already cleared up a lot since you got here. Besides, maybe he can see you've got potential." She dug a hole in her oatmeal. "Or maybe he's just bored."

"Whatever. It doesn't matter anyway. It's not like I'm ever going to see him again once I get out of here."

"Never say never," Jane said. "Lester and Grace met in here, and now look at them." She leaned forward. "And, Grace already had a boyfriend when she met Lester."

"I know," I said.

"What do you know?"

"I knew about them getting married here."

"How'd you know about that?"

"I saw them by the library the other day and they told me about it. How they were wild and crazy in love so they snuck out through the hole in the fence to go get married in Baton Rouge."

"You see!" She pointed at me, her fingers in the shape of a gun. "The hole!"

"Yep. Just like you said."

"Maybe the reason you got Hansen's disease was so that you would come here and meet Steve."

"Scott."

"Close enough."

"I don't think—"

"Maybe that was God's plan for you, for everything to happen just as it has because of a grand design that we can't see or understand."

"I don't believe that," I said.

"Well, maybe that doesn't matter."

"Okay. What's the reason you got Hansen's disease, then? What's the grand design there?"

She shrugged. "I don't know yet."

I took tiny bites of my oatmeal, trying not to gag on the sticky clumps.

"Maybe there's more than one reason," Jane said.

"Can you name one?"

"Well, I think it's made me more compassionate toward other people, for sure. When before I'd just be, like, whatever, not my problem, now I feel like I can actually empathize with people who are sick or injured or have experienced a profound loss."

"Big deal," I said. "What does compassion get you? A bleeding heart, that's all."

"It's about becoming more fully human, Abby."

"Look at me." I spread my arms. "I'm already a human. I'm not going to get any more human than this."

"You know that's not what I mean."

"Actually, I don't. I don't know what you mean at all."

"Look," Jane said. "All I'm saying is, we got Hansen's disease for a reason. Now it's up to us to figure out the reason."

"There is no *reason*, Jane! It was just a freak thing. It was being in the wrong place at the wrong time and being in the five percent of the population that's not immune to the bacteria!"

She shook her head sadly.

"The only reason you're saying there has to be a reason for it is because it's easier to think that. It's more comforting to think that it's all part of a greater plan that all makes sense to someone, somewhere, because it sure as shit doesn't make any sense when you're living it."

"What do you want, Abby?"

"I want . . . I want to be allowed to be mad. And sad. And frigging . . . devastated. This is the worst thing that's ever happened to me, okay? And it doesn't help me feel better for you to say that it happened for a reason. That's, like, the opposite of helping me."

"Okay . . ."

"Okay?"

"I won't say it anymore if you don't want me to."

"I don't!"

"Are you talking to Rodriguez today?"

"I don't know."

"Might be a good idea." Jane finished the last sip of her coffee and collected her dishes. "I'll see you later, alright?"

I nodded as she left me alone at the table, staring into the abyss of my oatmeal.

With a morning like that, there's not much hope for the rest of the day. It was Saturday so there was no bus to the clinic in Baton Rouge. I was trapped inside the 336 acres that was the National Hansen's Disease Museum, a.k.a., Carville. Which, did I mention? Was ACTUALLY a prison in the late 1990s. I was irritable and restless. I wanted OUT! I wanted to go shopping, see my friends, go to a party. But I couldn't do anything. Because I was a leper.

Scott wasn't even around for me to have someone to talk to. The cadets had gone on a day trip to go feed orphans or something. I don't know. They were all gone and the place was eerily quiet and empty without their green and khaki-ness filling it up. Dr. Rodriguez would come up to Carville to counsel us, but we had to book the appointment in advance, and I hadn't. I was so desperate for something to do that I actually did schoolwork. I wasn't sure if I was even going to pass my senior year or not, but I figured I might as well try. I had brought all my textbooks with me and a few assignments that had no real deadline. I was planning on taking my final exams, even if I had to do them from a hospital bed. High school is the kind of thing you only want to have to do once. Although, if Jane was right, I'd be doing it over and over again for the rest of my life.

I got through two chapters of my math textbook, had a long nap, and then woke up and finished one assignment for English. It was dinnertime by then, but I didn't feel like eating. I wanted to go to sleep so I could wake up to a new day and leave this one behind me.

Sometimes I wake up in a bad mood and it just gets worse and worse as the day goes on. I don't know why. It happened to me before I got leprosy too, obviously. But the bad moods seemed worse now that I was living with the black cloud of Hansen's disease dumping a shit-storm on my head day in and day out. Like now when I was in a bad mood, it was *really* bad. I knew I was a total hag to be around. And no amount of chocolate or ice cream or *America's Next Top Model* could shake me out of it. All I could do was go to bed and hope that when I woke up in the morning I would discover that it had all been a terrible dream. That I was still healthy. That I was still beautiful. That I had never heard of Hansen's disease. Or sulfone therapy. Or Carville, Louisiana.

But that morning never came.

The next day was Sunday. Visitor's day. I don't think I've ever been so excited to see my parents. I cleaned my room, dressed up and did my hair in a French braid. When I opened the door to air out my room, Jane passed by. She wore a purple dress and gold sparkly sandals.

"Hey, Abby."

"Hey, Jane."

We stared at each other in the white sunlight.

"Look," I said. "I'm sorry about yesterday. I was . . ."

She waved my words away. "You could be right," she said. "It is easier to believe that there's somebody who has a plan. Somebody who knows what's going on with everything. With everybody."

I nodded.

"Because I sure as hell don't!"

We laughed.

"It might be easier," she said. "But it's what I believe."

"Fair enough," I said.

She looked me up and down. "You going to church?" she said.

"Me? No."

"How come you're all dressed up then?"

"My parents are coming."

"Aw, that's cute."

I shrugged.

"Okay. I'm going to talk to God," Jane said. "See you later."

"Put in a good word for me."

She winked at me, gave me a little finger-wave, then clacked down the stairs, the skirt of her dress flouncing as she went. Then Barry came out of his room, which was next to Jane's. He wore a white T-shirt with a pink stain over the left nipple and gray sweatpants.

"Hi, Barry," I said.

"Good morning, Abigail," he said.

I snorted a bit.

Barry looked at me.

"No, it's nothing," I said, waving my hand. "It's just that no one has called me that in a long time," I said. "Sometimes I forget that's even my name."

"I know what you mean," he said.

I stared at him. The sun bounced off his bald spot and his glasses were dirty.

"Barry isn't my given name either. It's a short form," he said.

"What's it short for?"

He swallowed. "Bartholomew," he said.

I nodded. "Well, then, good morning, Bartholomew."

A smile flickered on his face for a moment and for a split second, I could almost see what he had looked like as a little boy. He nodded and passed by me, taking the steps slowly and deliberately, the way we'd been taught, holding onto the handrail with his mitten-hand.

I figured that Barry was one of those people who knew there was no reason for anything, and the unbearable desperation of that knowledge had taken its toll. For some reason I got the impression that getting Hansen's disease wasn't the worst thing that had ever happened to Barry. He had given up hope long ago.

I turned away from him and looked out over the field. Three people approached. I knew them by the way they walked. Mom and Dad had brought Dean with them, as a surprise, I guess. And I can tell you this for sure, I had never been so excited to see Dean before. I ran to them and hugged Dean first.

"Um," he said, putting his arms around me woodenly. "Hi."

"Dean! It's okay! I'm not contagious anymore! I'm on the cell-phone drugs, see."

"Okay," he said, half-chuckling. "Good to know."

I hugged Mom and Dad and thanked them for coming and told them how glad I was that they had made the trip.

"We drove up yesterday," Dad said. "So we could spend the whole day with you today."

I hugged him again, my eyes filling with tears.

When you're seventeen, your parents can annoy the living buck out of you. But, if I'm honest with myself, they really are the best. They're the only people you can count on to stick by you when things go sideways. And even though you treat them like sub-humans 90 percent of the time, they'll still show up early on visitor's day.

I don't remember too much about what we said or did that day. We walked around a lot. It was a nice day. The sky was clear and blue. I was feeling pretty good. I showed them the hole in the fence. Dean was unusually quiet and didn't even say anything jerky. Probably because Mom and Dad had threatened to run him over on the way out of the parking lot if he did.

We all had lunch together in the mess hall. Mom and Dad and Dean sat at the reserved table with me, Jane, Grace, Lester and Barry. It was like my real family and my leper family all dining together. Scott looked over at us, gave me a big smile and waved. I waved back.

Dean followed my gaze. "That your boyfriend?"

I shrugged. "Maybe one day."

"Hm," he said. "Cute."

I grinned. Mom looked sidelong at Dean. Dad was in conversation with Lester so I don't think he heard.

"What's going on at school?" I said.

"The usual BS," Dean said. He took a bite of his sandwich. "Carrie Nelson's pregnant."

"No!" I choked a little bit on my apple.

"Yup."

"Holy crap! Is it . . . Jude's?"

"Presumably."

"Whoa. Is she going to keep it?"

"I don't know."

"Shiiit."

"Your old buddy Liz is dating that weird skater guy."

"Nate Russell?"

"I guess." Dean chewed his sandwich, talking out of the side of his mouth. "She's gone kind of freaky too. Dyed her hair black and wears ripped-up clothes with safety pins stuck everywhere." He took a sip of his milk. "She looks alright, though. If you like voodoo dolls."

"What about Marla?"

"Same."

I nodded. "Has anyone asked about me?"

"Yeah, a few people."

I stared at him.

"Oh, who?"

"Yeah . . ."

"Um, let's see. That kid who lives near us . . ."

"Dustin?"

"Yeah. Him."

"Who else?"

"Uh . . . Coach Clayton. Let's see. Um, Aaron asked about you."

"That's it?"

"Yeah. Well, Rihanna Pilansky was there when Coach Clayton asked, but she didn't ask about you *herself*, so, I don't think she counted."

"Okay."

I didn't know whether to be happy that Dustin had asked about me or depressed because Marla and Liz hadn't. I was feeling both things at the same time. "And what did you tell them?"

"That you're sick and you've gone out of state for treatment." Dean shrugged.

"And do they . . . do they know what I'm sick *with*?"

He shook his head. "I haven't told anybody."

"Not even Aaron."

"Nope."

"Thanks," I said.

"You're welcome."

It was maybe the nicest thing Dean had ever done for me, not telling. I knew that it might get out eventually, but for now, no one outside my family knew, and I was comforted by that.

Grace and Lester and Jane said their goodbyes and nice-to-meet-yous and left the table. Barry nodded and shuffled off, back to his own private hell. But the four of us stayed at the table because Mom was still eating. My mom is the slowest eater in Texas and maybe even the whole world.

"Auntie Karen says hi," Dad said.

"Oh, thanks. Hi back."

"She wanted to send you some peanut butter brownies, but we didn't know if they allowed outside food in."

"Wait. Does Auntie Karen know why I'm here?"

Mom and Dad looked at each other.

I groaned. "She does, doesn't she?"

"We had to tell her, honey," Mom said. "She's our family. She cares about you."

"Who else did you tell?"

"That's it," Dad said. "The only people who know are us and Auntie Karen. And your doctors. But that's all."

"Swear to me you won't tell anyone else. Please."

"We won't," said Mom. "But you don't need to be ashamed, Abby. It's just a bacteria. You didn't do anything wrong. This could happen to anyone."

"Yeah. It happened to me. And I don't want to advertise it, okay?"

Mom wrinkled her eyebrows at me.

"*Please*, Mom!"

Dad squeezed her shoulder.

"Okay." She sighed. "Whatever you want."

"No one. Not a living soul."

"It's our secret, Abby. You don't have to worry about that," Dad said.

"You especially." I pointed at Dean.

He put his hands up.

"Swear on your life," I said.

"I swear on my life," he said. "I won't tell anyone you're a leper."

"Hansen's disease patient," I said.

"Same thing."

"No, it's not."

It wasn't the same thing, I realized. It wasn't the same at all.

After lunch, we played bocce with an ancient set that had probably been there since Grace and Lester's early days. We all goofed around except for Mom, because she gets so serious about games and has to win everything.

"I really want to come home next weekend," I said as they walked me back to my apartment.

"We know you do, sweetie. But you have to stay here until the four weeks are over," Mom said.

"Just for a visit. Not to stay."

"Oh," Mom said. She looked at Dad.

"I really miss you guys," I said. "And there are some things I need to take care of. With school. And cheerleading."

"I don't think you'll be doing cheer anymore, honey, I'm sorry to say," Dad said.

I explained to them about the USC scholarship. How getting it depended on my officially being part of the team. "Even if they could make me an assistant, a water girl, a mascot, *anything*, I'd still have a shot at USC for the fall."

Mom and Dad looked at each other, wary.

"*Please*," I said. "I have to try. And I have to speak to Coach Clayton about it in person."

"Abby," Dad said. "You have a very serious illness."

"I *know* that, Dad."

"Your health is the number one priority right now."

"But—"

"Not high school graduation. Not this USC scholarship. And certainly not cheerleading."

"But—"

"We have to face the fact that you may not even graduate this year, Abby," Mom said gently.

"But I have to try."

Mom and Dad looked at each other. Dean stared at his shoes, smudging the toe of one with the other foot. "She's right," Dean said, looking up. "You have to at least let her try."

Dad sighed.

"We'll have to get the okay from Dr. Mike first," Mom said.

"Of course."

"And you need to be home resting. Not going out with your friends all weekend."

"Oh, thank you, thank you, thank you!" I gave them both hugs around the neck and gave Dean a little thumbs-up. As nasty as he could be sometimes, he was there for me, my brother. When I needed him most, he had my back.

My family left not long after that to do the long drive home. Mom had brought me more homework assignments and a Shopaholic novel she had picked out for me from the used bookstore in our neighborhood, plus a new tube of lip gloss and a little bottle of pink nail polish, which meant more to me than she'll ever know.

I could get used to feeling weak and I could get used to the numbness in my hands and feet, but the thing that I hadn't gotten used to, and maybe never would, was not feeling pretty anymore. Maybe you think that's incredibly vain, fine. But when your total net worth, I mean all of your social currency, is wrapped up in your appearance, the things it can get you, the things it can do for you, and then you lose that, what have you got? Buck-all, that's what. Zero, zilch, nada. You're ugly, worthless and desperate, just like the freaks and fatties at school that you used to make fun of, only they never had it in the first place so they don't know how much it kills to lose it. And you wonder how you could have been such an unbelievable asshole to them just because of how they looked. On top of everything else, being on the other side makes you think about who you really were before. And let's just say, I was not a good Samaritan.

On Monday morning when the bus arrived at the clinic, the first thing I did was book an appointment with

Dr. Mike so I could get permission to go home for the weekend. When I saw him the following day he said he'd already talked to my mom and it should be fine as long as I took it easy and didn't forget to take the pills and keep up with my exercises. I thanked him and went out into the hallway to call Mom at work. She'd already booked my Greyhound ticket. I would leave Friday afternoon at 4:00 p.m. from the bus depot in Baton Rouge and get in around midnight. The bus back to Carville left Sunday at noon. It was a lot of riding the bus for a short amount of time at home, but I didn't care. I wanted out of Carville. Even if it was only for one day. Sometime Saturday or Sunday morning, I had to talk to Coach Clayton. I thanked my mom and told her I loved her and hung up.

My second week at Carville went by slower than the first. There was more physio: picking up towels with my toes, rolling out my feet on a foam roller, squeezing the stress ball until I wore the mouth off the happy face.

On Wednesday, I met with Dr. Rodriguez again. This time, she wanted to talk about the future. My future.

"I don't know what to tell you," I said. "It's all up in the air right now."

"Ideally," she said. "What would you like to see happen?"

I thought for a minute while I stared at the rocket-ship poster. "I'd like to go back in time and not eat armadillo meat," I said.

"We can't go back, Abby. Only forward."

"Unless we have a time machine," I said.

"That's right," she said. "But I'm guessing you don't."

I scuffed the toe of my shoe against the chair. "Right."

"So, let's talk about the next couple of months and the coming year. What do they hold for you, ideally?"

"I'd like to graduate," I said. "I'd like to go to my grad ceremony. I know there's not a snowball's chance in hell of being prom queen now, but, I'd like to at least go to my prom."

She nodded. "Okay. Good. Anyone in particular you'd like to go to the prom with?"

I shook my head, shrugging miserably.

"You don't have a—"

"No."

"Okay," she said. "That's okay."

"Everyone probably already has their date," I said.

"Your prom's in June?"

I nodded.

"That's still months away, Abby. Lots of time."

"Yeah, but I can't even go if I don't graduate. Plus, I don't want to go looking like this." I pointed to my face.

"There's a good chance the spots on your face will be cleared up by then. They're already looking better."

"Really?"

"I can't promise anything, but, like I said, there's a good chance."

I squeezed my eyes shut tight. "That would be awesome."

"And when do you expect to find out if you're going to graduate?"

"Not until June."

"Okay." She nodded. "And you've been keeping up with your studies? Doing your homework and all of your assignments?"

"I've been trying," I said.

"Good. So let's suppose you do graduate, then what?"

"I'd been hoping to go to USC in Los Angeles to study acting, but I can't go unless I get a full scholarship. It's a cheerleading scholarship, so it's contingent on me staying on the squad, and the coach writing me a letter of recommendation."

"I see," Dr. Rodriguez said.

"Except it looks like that's not going to happen anymore because, well, obviously I can't do stunts or really too much physically demanding activity right now. Maybe not ever again . . ."

"And have you talked to your coach about this?"

"Not yet. That's why I'm going back to Texas this weekend. To talk to her in person."

"That's good, Abby," Dr. Rodriguez said. "That shows real initiative."

"Thanks."

"But here's my question: if you *do* get the cheerleading scholarship to USC, won't you be expected to be a cheerleader for them?"

"I guess so, yeah."

"And if you can't cheer for them, will you be able to keep attending the university?"

"I . . . I don't know."

"I see. So even if you *do* graduate, even if you *do* get the scholarship, you might not be able to keep studying at USC if you can't cheer."

I nodded. "Basically, I'm screwed. Whatever happens, I'm screwed. That's the bottom line."

"Not necessarily," she said. "We just need to come up with a plan B."

"THERE IS NO PLAN B!"

Dr. Rodriguez sat back in her chair, startled.

"This has been the plan for as long as I can remember and there's nothing else I want to do and there's nowhere else I want to go!"

She held up her hands. "Okay."

"I don't even *like* cheerleading! I just did it so I could get the stupid scholarship!" I laughed. "I'm such an idiot. All those hours of practice, the cheer camps, entire weekends . . . wasted. And for what?"

"I'm sure it wasn't all a waste, Abby."

"It will be if I can't get into USC." Tears blurred my vision.

Dr. Rodriguez drummed her fingertips against the desk. "I think we should speak to someone at the university to confirm. Maybe I'm wrong. Maybe they won't require you to be on the squad there."

"I really hope you're wrong." My voice was tiny and far away. The present sucked balls, and the future wasn't looking any better.

The next day, Dr. Rodriguez helped me figure out who at USC could answer my question. She let me use the phone in her office and gave me some privacy. After waiting on hold for what felt like an hour, I finally got through to the right person. It turned out that if you get the scholarship, they expect you to cheer for them, just like Rodriguez had said. But all I could do was cling to the hope that I would somehow, some way be able to do it—in some capacity—but first I had to actually get the scholarship.

Scott and I went for a walk that night and I told him I was going home for a visit on the weekend.

"Lucky," he said. "They don't let us leave."

"You went on that field trip."

"Not the same."

"How much longer are you here for?"

"Two more weeks," he said, kicking a rock. "Then home to face the music."

"Hey," I said. "It could be worse. You could have leprosy."

We laughed. "Well, when you put it that way . . ."

We walked through a grove of old, mossy oaks, their knotted limbs reached up to the sky like tentacles. An owl hooted above us, and Scott closed his hand around mine. I was so surprised, I didn't know what to say, so I said nothing, just stared straight ahead, hoping he couldn't see the crimson blush creep over my face.

"Is this okay?" he said.

"Yep," I said.

"Okay. Good."

I smiled, looking at him from the corner of my eye.

"I like hanging out with you," he said.

"Me too."

"I can't hang out with any of my old friends when I get back home," he said.

"Why not?"

"For some of them, it's part of their probation that they can't hang out with me."

"Oh."

He ground his jaw. "They all have criminal records. Two of them have court dates coming up."

"That's rough," I said.

"I wish you lived in Oklahoma City. Then at least I'd have one friend."

"We could talk on the phone," I said.

"Yeah . . . I'm not very good on the phone. It's so . . . phony."

I laughed. "Maybe we could visit each other," I said. "Do you have a car?"

"No. But I could steal one."

"Really?"

"No!"

I laughed. "Right. Yeah. Don't do that. You wouldn't want to end up in . . ."

"A place like this?"

"Exactly."

He shrugged, gave me the side-eye. "It has its perks."

"Besides," I said. "Aren't you supposed to be all reformed after this program?"

He smirked. "I guess we'll find out in two weeks."

We didn't say anything for a while, just walked along, holding hands, and it was really, really nice.

"Are you going to your prom?" I asked.

"Oh hell no. I hate that shit."

"Oh."

"Why? Are you going to yours?"

I shrugged. "Probably not. I doubt anyone will ask me."

"Couldn't you go with a friend or something?"

"Not really."

"Why not?"

I sighed. "My friends . . . turned out to be not such good friends," I said.

"I hear that," said Scott.

"When I needed them most, they stopped talking to me. Pretended I didn't exist."

"Do you want me to beat them up?" Scott asked.

I laughed. "Kind of."

"Give me their addresses. It shall be done."

"No."

"You sure? It's no problem."

"Yeah." I laughed. "It's okay."

"We could pull a Carrie at your prom. Dump pig's blood all over everyone."

"It wasn't Carrie who did that. It was the mean kids who did it to her."

"Oh yeah. Carrie burnt it all down."

"Right."

"Well, we could do that too."

"I don't really feel like getting charged with arson."

"It's no big deal," he said. "Until you're eighteen, nothing sticks anyways."

"Scott?"

"Yeah, Tex?"

"How come you hate prom?"

"Because it's stupid! Everyone spends way too much money on clothes they'll never wear again, they drink too much, make fools of themselves, and make poor choices like driving drunk and having sex without a condom. Proms are just disasters waiting to happen. Plus all that king and queen bullshit. What is that? Oh, you're so popular and gorgeous so I'm going to vote for you so that you can wear a stupid plastic crown on your already too-big head? Come on."

"But . . . You only get one prom. Aren't you afraid you might regret not going?"

"Not a chance. I've been to one. It was one too many."

"Oh," I said. I scratched the back of my neck, letting go of his hand.

"This girl I knew was in twelfth grade last year. She took me as her prom date. It was embarrassing. She made me wear this hideous baby-blue tux, hang out with all her annoying friends—"

"I see."

"Look, it was a really fucked-up night, okay?"

"Okay," I said.

"I don't like to talk about it."

"We don't have to talk about it."

"But I want to tell you. I feel like I should tell you."

"Okay."

He sighed. "She ended up getting really smashed that night. I mean, *super* drunk."

I nodded.

"There were these guys at the party . . . They're not my friends. I knew them, a few of them, but they weren't my friends." He crossed his arms over his chest. "They got her upstairs. I saw her going up there with them. I mean, she was still talking and walking and everything. She said she was okay." He shrugged. "So I didn't do anything. I didn't stop her or anything. Just went back to playing beer pong like a total asshole."

I bit my lip.

"So. Anyways. Long story short. Whatever happened upstairs got her so messed up that she killed herself two weeks later."

"Holy shit." My hand flew over my mouth. "I'm so sorry, Scott. That's . . . that's terrible."

"Worst part is?" He pointed to his chest. "I could have stopped it."

"It's not your fault," I said.

"But it kind of is though. Or close enough."

I didn't know what to say.

"Everyone knew I was her prom date. That she was basically my responsibility that night. And did I ever fuck that up royally. After she died, people treated me like a total . . ."

"Leper?"

He let out a short laugh. "Yeah, you could say that."

"I'm really sorry, Scott."

He rubbed his hand over his face. "It is what it is. Maybe part of the reason I hate prom so much."

We were quiet for a moment.

"Look, I don't know why I told you that. I wasn't going to tell you. It just kind of . . . came out. Please don't hate me, Abby."

"I don't hate you," I said.

"You don't? You should. I'm a total fuck-head."

"Everyone makes mistakes."

"Yeah. You probably don't."

I laughed. "I think maybe the last five years of my life were a mistake. Maybe my whole life. Definitely all of high school."

He smiled a tiny bit. "Thank you." He took my hand again and squeezed it gently in his.

The moon was a silver teardrop shining down on us. We headed back to my apartment then, and I thought about how there are so many things that can go wrong in a life, so many things that are unfair, that are awful. And the older you get, the more sad things there are.

I gave Scott a long hug good night. We didn't say anything, just held on tight like we were trying to keep each other from breaking apart.

When I got back to my room I started getting ready for bed, but I couldn't get Carrie Nelson out of my mind. I lay awake half the night thinking about her. She was in twelfth grade and pregnant with Jude Mailer's baby. What was she going to do? What were they going to do? I had assumed Carrie and Jude would be smart enough to use protection. But then, I hadn't with Chad. That could've been me right now, pregnant. *God.* I don't know what the hell I would've done. Luckily, that was one thing I didn't have to worry about. My life may have been completely screwed up, but my period was as regular as ever. Would I trade places with Carrie right now if I could? So she could have Hansen's disease and I could be pregnant with Jude's baby? I don't know. I realized that Carrie wouldn't be able to be on the cheer team this year either. It would be too risky; if she fell, the baby . . . But instead of feeling smug about that, I just felt bad for her. I knew Carrie loved cheerleading. Probably more than me, Marla and Liz combined, and now she wouldn't get to cheer in her senior year. For a good long while after Jude dumped me, I hated Carrie. I mean, *really* hated her, wished bad things for her, scowled at her in the halls, called her awful names behind her back, all that. But now that I was at Carville, everything felt different. I didn't hate her at all. Or wish anything bad for her. I felt sorry for her and I wished there was something I could do to help her. Maybe she and Jude would get married. Doubtful, but it could happen. I hoped that whatever happened, it would be the best-case scenario. For both of them. There was no great option, of course, but I hoped that whatever decision Carrie and Jude made, they wouldn't hate each other for it, wouldn't regret it for the rest of their lives.

Scott and I hung out the next day too. During his free period we went to the old canteen, which had been turned into a games room. There was a pool table, shuffle board and a bunch of ancient board games stacked along the walls.

He picked up a pool cue and surveyed the table. "Looks like this pool table has been here since the dinosaurs roamed the Earth."

The green felt was all chewed up and the legs were scratched and gouged.

"Are you trying to find excuses before we start?" I said.

"Rack 'em up," he said.

So I did.

We were tied two—two and then we had the rubber match. The last game was really close, but Scott ended up sinking the eight ball when he still had the six on the table.

"Nooooo!" he yelled and mimed flinging his cue against the wall.

"Victory is mine!" I held my cue in both hands and raised it over my head, turned a little circle.

"I bow to you, goddess of billiards." He got down on one knee and lowered his head.

"As you must," I said.

"Give me another chance tomorrow?" he said as he stood up, brushing the dust off his pants.

"If you're good," I said.

"I'm not good," he said. "But I'm lucky." He grinned at me.

"We'll see about that."

It was fun, being with him. For a short while, I could even forget where I was, and why I was there. But as soon as we stepped outside, the spell was broken.

Lester and Grace kept chickens and a Tom turkey behind their cottage and the turkey had gotten out. They were both chasing after him, their arms outstretched, stumbling around blindly. The bird seemed to know they couldn't see him and would move just out of reach as they approached. Scott and I turned to each other. His mouth turned up at the corner and then we both burst out laughing.

"Don't just stand there guffawing!" Lester yelled at us. "Help us get him back!"

When you get up close to a turkey, they're actually kind of scary looking. Their skin is all bumpy and red. And they're bigger than you'd think. They look kind of demonic. A turkey could probably really hurt you if it wanted to. Scott and I approached cautiously.

"What do you want us to do?" Scott called.

"Catch the darned thing before an alligator gets to it!" Grace said.

Scott lunged for the turkey and it flapped away. I laughed. He lunged for it again and it hopped out of reach. I laughed harder. He turned to me. "Don't laugh! It's hard!" He tried a third time and still the turkey got away. "How do you catch him?" he called to Lester.

"Grab his tail feathers!" Lester called.

"Get him by the legs!" Grace said.

He tried for a while longer while I covered my mouth with both hands so he couldn't see me laughing. Finally, Scott got a hold of the turkey's legs and was able to hold him.

"Oh good!" Grace said. "He's got him."

"How did you know that?" I asked her.

"The sound," she said, pointing to her ear.

"What do you want me to do with him?" Scott said.

"Put him back behind the fence," said Lester.

Scott heaved the turkey over the fence and it flapped to the ground, squawking.

"Thank you, son," Lester said.

"Great job!" said Grace, chuckling.

"You're welcome," Scott said, wiping his brow. He turned to me, smiled. "Shall we?" he said.

I giggled and took his arm. We started back toward my apartment.

"That was amazing," I said.

"Oh, yeah? You liked that?"

"You must be the best turkey catcher in all of Oklahoma," I said. "Maybe the best in the Midwest."

"I reckon it wasn't too bad for my first time."

"That was your first time? No! I don't believe it. You're a natural!"

"Hey now," he said. "I didn't see you going after that bird."

"How could I have? I didn't want to steal your thunder. Especially after beating you so badly at pool."

"It was kind of fun, actually."

"Maybe he'll get out again tomorrow and you can do it all over again."

"Here's to hoping."

I laughed.

"What are you doing now?" he said as we stood in front of the steps to my apartment.

I checked the time on my phone, stifled a yawn. "I should probably take a nap," I said. "All that turkey catching and pool winning really took it out of me."

"Okay," Scott said. "Well, I'll see you later, I guess."

"Okay," I said.

He gave me a little salute and walked away. I smiled all the way up to my room and was still smiling as I got into bed and pulled the covers over me.

Jane razzed me that night at dinner. "Carville," she said. "Higher match-making success rate than Tinder."

I rolled my eyes.

"Sooo, how was your date? Tell, tell, tell." She squeezed my arm.

"It wasn't a date, Jane. We're not dating. We're just friends."

"Honey. You and I are friends. That boy is actively pursuing your ass."

Barry looked over at us, his eyes wide and gooey behind his glasses.

"Shut up," I whisper-yelled.

"Well, it's true. Just look at him."

We looked across the cafeteria to where Scott was sitting. Other guys surrounded him. They were all talking, laughing, being loud, joking around. But Scott just sat there quietly amongst them, staring at me.

"Oh no," I said and put my face in my hands.

"Oh yes," Jane said. "He's got it bad for you."

Barry craned his neck, trying to see Scott.

"I believe the word is . . . twitterpated," Jane said. Then she let out one of her big rowdy laughs that seemed to shake the whole room.

"But how can he . . . ? Why would he even . . . ? I'm . . . "

"Don't think too much, Abby. You might hurt yourself," Jane said.

I gave her the finger and she laughed at me.

"No, but seriously, Jane. What am I going to do?"

She patted me on the shoulder. "I'm sure you'll think of something."

When Friday finally came I was so excited. I was going home! Just for a day and a half, but still. Home! After I got back from the clinic, I packed my bag for the weekend and then looked around for Scott to say goodbye to him, but I couldn't find him anywhere. Jane walked me to the front gates where my cab was waiting.

"Be good," she said, hugging me. "Don't do anything I wouldn't do."

I waved to her as the taxi drove away and she blew me a kiss.

There were a lot of people waiting at the bus station in Baton Rouge. A couple with two loud-mouthed little kids. An old guy with a white beard and icy blue eyes. A lady with a green sequined purse. A few of them eyed me warily as we lined up to get on the bus. I wondered if they could tell I was coming from Carville. If it was obvious. I got my makeup kit out of my bag and put on some lip gloss. Then the driver called out, "FIVE MINUTES!" and people started loading their luggage underneath. I put my makeup kit away and stood in line. The bus driver checked my ticket and asked for my ID. My heart leapt into my throat. Was I on a no-fly list? Was I not allowed to ride transit because of the disease? Would I be turned away once he saw the name on my ID? I pulled my license out of my wallet, my hands shaking. The bus driver glanced at it then looked back at me. "Welcome aboard," he said.

"Thanks," I said. My shoulders relaxed. I climbed the steps up to the bus carefully, holding on to the rail with both hands. This was not the time to turn an ankle. Plus, how embarrassing would it be to fall getting on the bus?

Once I got to my seat I pulled up my hood and spread my bag and coat out on the seat beside me so no one would sit next to me. Probably if they thought I was coming from Carville, no one would have sat next to me anyway. It was a long ride but I slept for a lot of it, and I had tons of music and games on my phone so it wasn't so bad.

Finally, we pulled into the ████████ station. Dad was there waiting for me. He gave me a hug and then took my bag. We got in the car and drove home.

"How are you doing, Abby?" Dad said.

"I've been better."

"Yeah." He stared out the windshield. He looked so sad in that moment—I think the word is *forlorn*—I had to say something else, something to comfort him.

"I'm okay though. I've made a couple of friends."

He looked over at me. "That's great, sweetie. That's really, really great."

"Well," I said, shrugging. "It helps, anyway."

"I'm sure it does."

We stopped at a red light and I could feel him looking at me. I wondered what he was thinking; I wondered if I grossed him out. I stared down at my hands. I pinched the end of each of my fingertips and felt nothing. Soon, we pulled into our driveway.

"Here we are," Dad said.

"Home sweet home."

He smiled at me and helped me into the house with my bags.

Dean was watching an old black and white movie on TV and Mom was knitting a yellow scarf. They both jumped off the couch when I walked in the door and came to hug me. It was already midnight so we didn't stay up too late. Mom made me some toast and tea, and then I went to bed. It had never felt so good to sleep in my own bed. I lay awake for a long time listening to the familiar noises of my house. The water running in Mom and Dad's bathroom as they got ready for bed, the click-clack of Dean's keyboard, and the buzzes and hums of the heat and lights. I had never really noticed these sounds before. But that night, I savored them.

I had a weird dream that I was back on the bus and the other passengers were all the guys I had ever liked or kissed or anything: Scott; Chad; Jude; Dustin; Mr. Neal, our hot chemistry teacher; even Anthony, my fourth grade boy-friend, was there. I sat at the back of the bus and looked at the backs of their heads, then they all turned around and started booing me. Chad threw a plastic bag full of condoms at me and Jude threw a basketball at my head. Mr. Neal threw a petri dish. I ducked so none of it hit me, but I was so upset. I crawled under my seat, covered my head with my arms and started to cry. They kept throwing more things. Rotten fruit and underwear. A wad of gum on the bus floor got stuck to my face and I couldn't get it off. I was tearing at my face, trying to rip the gum off, but ripping my skin off instead. Then a hand reached out and touched me on the shoulder. I looked up. It was Jane. She had purple hair but I knew it was her.

"Jane! Help me!"

"What's wrong, Abby?"

"They hate me. They all hate me!"

"Why do they hate you?"

"Because . . . because I'm not pretty anymore. They hate that I'm so ugly."

She pulled me up onto the seat. Things kept flying at us. Spiral notebooks and khaki pants. A bag of marbles. More fruit. A stuffed dog. Death metal played full blast out of the bus speakers. It was so loud and so awful. "Abby." Jane turned my face toward hers, held my cheeks in both her hands. "There are more important things than being beautiful."

I stared at her. "Oh," I said. She nodded, took her hands away from my face. Then everything got quiet. The boys turned around. Stopped throwing things. Sunlight poured in the bus windows and caught little bits of dust and everything on the bus began to shimmer. I looked down at my hands. They were shimmering too. The bus driver whistled a tune I knew but couldn't remember the name of. It was the only sound.

The next morning I woke up and stared at the ceiling for a long time, remembering my dream. I hummed a little part of the bus driver's tune, trying to place it, but I still couldn't remember what the song was called or how I knew it. Finally, I got out of bed and took a long shower, enjoying every second of it, because the water pressure at Carville sucked. Then I blow-dried my hair and straightened it and did my makeup. When I came downstairs, my parents had a huge breakfast going. Banana pancakes, bacon, fresh-squeezed orange juice, cinnamon buns, coffee. All my favorites.

"You should come home every weekend," Dean said, crunching a piece of bacon.

"Aww, are you saying you miss me?"

"No. I miss bacon," he said.

"Well, I'm only there for two more weeks. Then I'll be back in your life again. Full-time."

"Can't wait," he said.

I gave him a sugary smile.

"Are you going back to school when you get back?" Dean asked.

I took a sip of my coffee, then set my mug down. "Yeah, for the last month and a bit I guess," I said.

"Aren't you going to be so screwed though?"

"It might be okay. As long as I pass all my finals, I should be able to graduate this year. I mean, I did pretty well on my SATs in the fall."

"You certainly did, honey," Mom said.

"No, I mean socially screwed," Dean said. "Because, you

know, you're not really allowed to hang out with the beautiful people anymore."

"*Dean*," Dad said, grinding his jaw. "Please."

I stared at Dean for a cold moment. "There are more important things than being beautiful," I said.

"Who are you and what have you done with my sister?"

"*Dean!*" Mom said.

I dug into my pancakes. He was right. I'd be bucked in the friend department for the rest of my senior year. But I was right too. Your priorities change when you get sick and when you get older. I was both.

We had a really fun day. Mom and Dad said we could do whatever I wanted to do. I picked bowling because I hadn't done it in a long time and I remembered that it was an excellent feeling to knock down all the pins and hear them crack and smash against each other. Dad let Dean drive because my dad is a crazy person. Mom and I sat in the back of the car. She put her arm around me. "It's so good to have you home," she said, squeezing my shoulder. "Maybe you should come home next weekend too."

"I'll see if I can," I said.

"I don't know what I'm going to do when you and Dean move out," Mom said.

"You're not going to trip over my shoes or find moldy plates in Dean's room," I said.

"Oh, I know," she said. "But it's coming so soon."

"July first," Dean said. "For me."

"Dean, are you sure you're going to be able to afford—"

"*Yes*, Dad."

"Okay. It's just that, you know, you don't have a job, so . . ."

"I *told* you guys, I've been playing online poker for years. I have a lot of savings." Dean cut his eyes at me in the rear-view mirror.

"Is that legal?" Mom said.

"Of course it's legal!" Dean said.

"But you're not twenty-one," Mom said.

"But it's *On. Line.*"

"But don't you still have to be—"

"It's all on the up and up, Mom. Don't even worry about that. Just worry about what you guys are going to do when you're bored empty-nesters and don't have me around for free entertainment."

"You were never free, honey," Mom said.

We all laughed.

"Reasonably priced entertainment," Dean said.

"Mm, that's a stretch," she said.

We laughed again.

Dean pulled into the parking lot of the bowling alley. I rented a pair of baby-blue bowling shoes that I loved wearing because

1) They were so pretty, and

2) They weren't my leper shoes

I bowled the best game of my life but didn't come close to winning. Mom kicked all of our asses by a mile because she's twinkle toes and doesn't know how to lose. Afterwards we went out for pizza and wings. Mom and Dad got a pitcher of beer and let Dean and I have half a glass each. It was a really good night. The best night I've had in a long, long time. For a few seconds there, I even forgot I had leprosy.

B efore I went to bed, I knocked on Dean's door. I could hear him shuffling around inside.

"Just a minute," he called. More shuffling. Some drawers banged shut.

I cleared my throat.

"Okay," he said. "What is it?"

I opened the door a crack. "Hi," I said.

"Hey, Abby. Uh, what's up?"

I stepped inside his room. "I just wanted to say good night," I said.

"Okay. Yeah. Good night." His computer monitor was off but he kept glancing at it.

"Are you still doing the . . . ?" I pointed to the computer.

"Yeah. Yep. Same old, same old." He laughed, nervous.

"And it's . . . okay? I mean, you're good with everything?"

"Oh, you know, it can get a little hairy."

I laughed.

"But, yeah, no. It's fine. For the most part . . ."

I nodded. "How's Aaron?"

He shrugged. "Don't know. We haven't hung out since he started dating that stupid Canadian chick."

"I'm sorry. That sucks."

"No, she's actually really smart. If he doesn't flunk senior year, it'll be because of her."

"Still sucks, though. Losing a friend like that."

"Well." He leaned back in his chair and put his hands behind his head. "I guess that makes two of us."

"Yeah." I looked down at the carpet. It was worn and gray from years of abuse.

"You doing okay?"

I sighed. "I think so. Mostly. You know, all things considered . . ."

He nodded. "That's good."

"I guess . . ."

"Abby, I know I never thanked you properly . . . for saving my life that day."

I shrugged.

"Thank you," he said.

I nodded. Stared at a stain on the carpet. "You would've done the same for me," I said.

"I don't think I could have," he said. "I never learned CPR."

"Well, you're welcome then."

"And thanks for not telling Mom and Dad about it."

"Okay. Well . . . Good night, Dean."

"Abby?"

"Yeah?"

"Nothing. Never mind. Good night." He smiled his lopsided grin at me and I smiled back. Then I closed his door softly behind me. It wasn't exactly "I love you," but it was the closest we ever got.

After another luxurious morning shower, I went downstairs. Mom and Dad had made another massive breakfast: scrambled eggs, sausages, waffles, fruit salad and cranberry muffins.

"Dean!" Mom shouted up the stairwell. "Breakfast!"

No response.

"Oh well," she said. "He'll be down in a minute. It's getting cold. Let's eat."

Dad dished out eggs onto everyone's plates. I poured myself a coffee and refilled Mom's coffee.

"Dean!" Dad yelled. "Your eggs are getting cold!"

"Will you go see what's taking him, Abby?" Mom said. "You might need to wake him up."

"Sure." I went upstairs and banged on Dean's door. "Breakfast time!" I waited a moment, then opened the door and stepped into his room.

His bed was made up neatly, which was not like him at all. And his backpack was gone. Oh, Christ. Was my brother enough of an idiot that he would go meet some stranger off the Internet? Yes, yes, he was. I turned on his computer. He had deleted his browser history, nothing was open, and I couldn't hack into his email. The hair on the back of my neck prickled and I got a leaden feeling in my stomach. In my seventeen years of knowing him, Dean had never once made his bed. Something was very wrong with this picture.

"Abby! Dean!" Mom called from the bottom of the stairs.

I took out my phone and dialed Dean's number. Straight to voice mail. I hung up. Shook my head. "What a dumbass," I said under my breath. I went downstairs and took my seat at the table.

"Dean's bed is made and his backpack is gone. Looks like he's gone off somewhere."

"Hm. That's odd," Dad said. "His bed was made?"

"I don't think that's ever happened," Mom said. "Did he have any plans that you know of?"

"Nope." I stabbed into a sausage.

"Strange," Mom said. "He didn't mention going any-where this weekend."

"He's been acting queer lately," Dad said, chewing thought-fully.

I choked a little bit on my sausage.

"There's something going on with him," Dad said.

"He has been pretty quiet lately," Mom said.

"Dean? Quiet? There must be something very wrong, then," I said.

They both looked at me. I chewed my food and stared at my plate. I wasn't hungry anymore, but I kept eating so I'd have something to do with my hands.

"What time is your meeting with your coach?" Mom asked.

"About an hour," I said.

"Need a ride?" Dad asked.

"I can drive. If I can borrow your car?"

"Are you sure?" Mom said.

"Yeah, I can still drive, Mom. I may have leprosy, but I can still drive."

They looked at each other. Dad nodded.

"Okay," she said. "If that's what you want to do."

"It is."

We finished breakfast and I helped Dad do the dishes. He didn't say much, but he ground his jaw the way he does when he's anxious about something.

"I'll see you later on, okay?" I said when it was time for me to go.

"Alright, kid. Hope it goes well." He gave me a small smile and drained the sink.

Both of their cars were in the garage, so wherever Dean had gone, he hadn't driven there. I cranked the radio on the way to meet Coach Clayton and tried to pump myself up by singing along, but there was no good music on any of the stations.

I met Coach Clayton at the coffee shop near our school. She sat at a small table near the window sipping a latte.

"Abby!" She beamed at me. "How are you?"

"I'm okay, Coach. How are you?"

"Good, good." She nodded. "Have a seat."

"I'll just grab a drink first," I said.

"Sure, sure."

I ordered an iced cappuccino and sat down across from Coach Clayton.

"So I understand you've had some medical issues lately," she said, eyeing the flaky red skin around my hairline.

"Yeah, um. That's what I have to talk to you about."

"Okay."

"So . . . because of my, um, medical issues, I'm not in the same physical shape as I was before . . ."

"I see."

"But I still really want to be on the squad."

"Um hm."

"I mean, I *need* to be on the squad, Coach."

"You need to be?"

"Yes!"

She sat back a little. "And why is that?"

I sighed. "Because I put all my eggs in one basket."

She took a sip of her coffee and waited for me to continue.

"If I'm not on the squad this year, I can't apply for the cheering scholarship at USC, which is the only school I want to go to. I want to study acting there and I don't have any other . . . I don't have a plan B."

Coach Clayton looked at me. I saw pity in her green eyes. "Abby—"

"I just wanted to talk to you to find out if I could be on the squad in some other capacity, water girl or . . . or mascot." I winced. "Something. Just while I'm recovering. Until I can get back to cheering."

"Abby, I hate to be the one to tell you this, but that scholarship is very, *very* competitive. Out of the hundreds of girls I know who have applied, not one of them has ever gotten it."

"But—"

"It would be pretty much impossible to get it if you weren't actually cheering. There's a video component."

"Oh." Tears bristled in my eyes.

"I think it's time you came up with a plan B," she said gently.

I wiped my eyes on the back of my sleeve. My heart weighed a thousand pounds. I nodded. Coach Clayton nodded back.

I knew she was right. But that had been my goal for so long it was hard to see any other possibilities. If I didn't go to

USC, I didn't know what the hell I was going to do. I knew I didn't want to stay in Texas, but I didn't know how to get out, either.

I took the bus back to Carville at noon. I tried calling Dean a bunch more times—straight to voice mail. Except the robot voice came on the third or fourth time I called and said the voice-mailbox was full. Mom and Dad had probably been leaving him messages. I texted him: call home ASAP.

What a moron, I thought, and stared out the window as the landscape got more and more soggy. *I'm sure he's fine though*, I tried to console myself. *He's probably just . . . with friends. But what friends?* I had no idea where he might've gone. And I wasn't sure I wanted to know. I just wanted to know that he was okay. I picked at my nails. I thought about telling Mom and Dad about his webcam thing. But I figured he'd probably get home any minute and everything would be fine. I decided to wait to tell them. I don't know why.

I pushed thoughts of Dean and all the terrible things that could be happening to him out of my head. I had to think about my future. After Carville. After graduation. What was I going to do with my life?

I rested my forehead on the seat in front of me. It was too big a question. And I had no answers. No ideas even. Plus every time I closed my eyes, I saw Dean being hacked to pieces by one of his hairy creep-o Internet clients. I started to feel really bad for my parents. Their daughter had leprosy and their son might be murdered by an Internet psycho. And what had they ever done to deserve it? Nothing.

I tried calling Dean again. When voice mail picked up, I hung up, turned my phone off and put it away. I needed to think. I needed to come up with a plan B. What did I even want for my life? I wanted to be famous. I wanted to be a household name. To be sought after. Asked for my autograph. But why? Why did I want that? What would it even prove? That I was beautiful? That I was talented? That I was a good person? And did any of that even matter anymore? All I really wanted at that moment was to regain my health, to go back to how I was before I got Hansen's disease and to see my brother alive again.

When I got back to Carville it was late and the grounds were a ghost town. The cadets were all squared away and no one else was around. The only movement came from the pecan trees swaying gently in the wind. The quiet was unnerving. Goose pimples rushed along my arms. I wanted to knock on Jane's door but I figured she was already asleep and I didn't want to wake her up. I went into my apartment. It smelled like donkey butt, so I opened the window and left the door propped open. As soon as I turned my phone on, it rang.

"Hi, Mom."

"Hey, honey. Did you get in okay?"

"Yep. I'm here."

"That's good. The bus ride was alright?"

"Uh-huh."

"Great. Hey, Abby?"

"Yeah?"

"Have you heard anything from Dean? He's not back yet."

"No."

"No texts? Nothing?"

"No. Sorry, Mom."

"Okay. Well. Do me a favor?"

"Yep."

"Let us know right away if you hear from him."

"I will," I said. "And you too. Let me know if you hear from him."

"Are you worried about him?" I could hear her throat constrict.

"No, I'm sure he's fine. He's a big boy," I said.

"He's just never done anything like this before. I know he's technically an adult, but it's—"

"It'll be okay, Mom." I didn't know for sure, but what else could I say?

"Yeah." I could hear the tears caught in her voice. "Well, you're probably tired. I'll let you go."

"Okay. Good night, Mom."

"Good night, sweetheart. Love you."

As soon as I hung up with her, I dialed Dean. Still straight to voice mail. Still a full mailbox. I hung up and got in the shower. I turned the water as hot as it would go and let it scald my shoulders and back.

When I got out of the shower, I watched in the mirror as the steam rose off my body. It looked like I was made entirely of mist and dissolving one water particle at a time. I combed my hair and brushed my teeth and got into bed. I left my phone on and charging beside the bed in case Dean tried to call.

I slept terribly and had dreams with blood and chains and dildos in them. When my alarm went off at 6:45 a.m., I was actually glad. I grabbed my phone. No texts. No missed calls. I got up and started to get ready. I carefully did my makeup and hair. I was excited to see Scott again. I hadn't realized it until that morning, but I had missed him.

I met Jane coming out of her apartment.

"Hey! Welcome back!" she gave me a hug.

"Thanks."

"How was it?"

"Good. Weird."

"Yeah, it always is."

I nodded.

"Breakfast?"

"Yeah."

We walked to the mess hall together, arms linked.

"What did I miss?" I said.

"Well, let's see . . . Grace gave me a rug-hooking lesson."

"Sounds thrilling."

"Oh, it was. Barry and I played checkers. Barry won."

"Wow, you must have been desperate for company."

"I was."

"Did he try to kiss you?"

"Ew! No!" She laughed. "No, he's actually a pretty interesting dude. Once he warms up to you."

"I'm not sure I want him to warm up to me," I said.

Jane shrugged. "Beggars can't be choosers."

"But I—"

"Look, you don't get to pick your family, right?"

"Right . . ."

"Well, you don't get to pick your Carville family either."

I picked a piece of lint off my sweater.

"We're all stuck here together for who knows how long. You might as well get to know the other people in your same predicament."

"Uh-huh."

"Like I said before, Abby, we're not all that different."

"Yeah. You and Barry are practically the same person."

She rolled her eyes. "Oh, go on with your snobbery."

I laughed.

On our way to our table, I saw Scott seated with the other cadets and my stomach floated up into my throat. I stopped near his table.

"I'll save your spot," Jane said, winking at me.

"Hey," he said, coming up to me.

"Hi."

"How was Texas?"

"Um . . ."

"That good, huh?"

"Do you have any free time today?"

"Yeah, right after breakfast."

"Can we . . . ?"

"Sure. I just finished eating. I'll wait for you by the lake."

"Okay."

He smiled at me. "See you in a bit."

"Yep." I nodded. I could feel myself blush. I don't know why I was blushing. It was embarrassing. I lowered my head and walked to the counter to pick up my food. I got cereal with fruit, orange juice and a coffee. I sat down beside Jane. Barry sat across from us. He nodded at us but didn't talk. He was reading an issue of *Scientific American*.

I rushed through my breakfast so that I could go meet Scott.

"Don't they feed you at home?" Jane said.

"I'm meeting Scott after this," I said.

She snorted. "Good thing he's not here to see you eat like this. He probably wouldn't want to be your boyfriend anymore."

"He's not my boyfriend."

"He is so. He's your Carville boyfriend," she said.

I gulped down my coffee, narrowed my eyes at her.

"She's right," Barry said.

We both stared at Barry.

"He's your Carville boyfriend." He flipped a page of his magazine, nonchalant. "It happens."

"Okay. Well . . . I guess that's settled then," I said.

Jane gave me bug eyes. I could tell she wanted to laugh but was holding it in.

"I'll see you later." I squeezed Jane's shoulder on my way past her. "Bye, Barry."

"Yep." He waved but didn't look up from his magazine.

On my way to the lake I got a text from Mom:

Any word from Dean?

I texted her back right away. First I typed No but then I erased it, tried to sound more optimistic:

Not yet.

I found Scott beside the lake. He stared into it like he was trying to see to the bottom.

"Hey." I tapped him on the shoulder.

"Oh." He gave a little start. "Hey." He hugged me quick then stood back. "How was your time at home?"

"Not great."

"Why? What happened?"

I sighed. "I talked to my coach. She basically told me there's no hope in hell of me ever getting the USC scholarship, so I can kiss that dream goodbye. And my brother—" Without warning, I began to cry. I didn't even know that I was going to cry. It just burst out. "Shit. Sorry." I wiped my eyes.

"It's okay," Scott said. "What about your brother?"

I laughed the kind of weird little laugh that happens in the middle of crying. "My brother has gone AWOL."

Scott raised his eyebrows.

"My parents haven't heard from him, he's not answering his phone, he's just . . . gone."

"Jeez . . ."

"Yeah."

"Did you call his friends? Ask if anyone's seen him?"

I bit my lip. Shook my head. "I should do that," I whispered.

He shrugged. "I would."

"You're a good person. You think of things like that." I had to work hard not to cry again. "I'm not."

"Abby, come on."

"I think about myself too much. I don't—" I couldn't stop the tears. They came hard and fast.

"Hey, hey. It's okay. It's going to be okay." He put his arms around me. "I'm sure your brother is fine. He probably just needed a break."

I pushed his arms away. "But how can you know that? How can you be so sure?"

He stepped back. "I'm not sure," he said. "It's just . . . the most likely scenario."

I shook my head. "I don't think so."

"I've taken off a few times before without telling anyone where I was."

"Really?"

"Yeah."

"For how long?"

"I don't know. A couple of days."

"What did you do?"

"Nothing much. Bummed around with some street kids downtown. Went to the skate park. Drank some beer. I just didn't want to go home . . . so I didn't."

"This is different," I said.

"Maybe. Maybe not."

"Dean is . . . he has a webcam business," I said.

"Like . . . selling webcams?"

"No. Like, *webcam* webcam."

"Oh," he said, scratching his chin. "Hm."

"Yeah."

"So . . . you think he went to meet someone from . . . ?"

"I don't know. I don't know what to think."

"I think you should call around. Ask some people. Someone probably knows something."

"Okay." I took a deep breath. "You're right. I'm going to do that."

He nodded, gave me a little smile. "I'm sorry but we have this drill thing. I have to be there. See you at lunch?"

"Yeah."

"Alright." He put his hands in his pockets and began to walk away.

"Hey, Scott?"

He turned back to me.

"Thanks."

He nodded, once, and continued walking.

I sat down beside the lake and took out my phone. I scrolled through my phonebook and stopped on Dustin Lorimer. He wasn't really Dean's friend, but he was Aaron's friend and would have Aaron's number. I had never called Dustin before. But I should have. Who cared if he was vanilla? My finger hovered above the screen for a moment. Then I pushed call. He answered right away.

"Hey, Dustin. It's Abby. Abby Furlowe."

"Oh, hey, Abby. How are you doing?"

"Um, okay. Thanks. How about you?"

"Pretty good. Pretty good."

"Sorry to bother you so early."

"It's no problem," he said.

"Thing is, Dean, my brother—" I choked up.

"Yeah?"

I held the phone away, coughed and cleared my throat. "Um, Dean's kind of gone AWOL and, so, I was just wondering if you had heard anything, where he might be, or I thought maybe Aaron would know, and I was hoping you could give me Aaron's number?"

"Hm. How long has he been gone for?"

"Uh, well, we saw him Saturday night. That was the last time . . ."

"Yeah, I haven't heard anything. I'm pretty sure he was at school on Friday. That's the last time I would've seen him."

"Okay," I said.

"Are you worried?"

"Well, yeah . . ."

"Sorry. Of course you're worried. I don't know why I asked that."

"It's okay," I said. "Do you have Aaron's number?"

"Yeah. For sure. I'll text it to you."

"Okay, thanks, Dustin."

"Hey, Abby?"

"Yeah?"

"When are you coming back to school?"

"As soon as I can," I said.

"Alright. Well, I guess I'll see you then."

"Yeah."

"Take care, Abby. I hope everything's okay with Dean."

"Thanks. Me too."

"Bye."

"Bye, Dustin."

I hung up. He had already texted me Aaron's number. I called Aaron. It rang for a while then went to his voice mail but the mailbox was full. My heart sped up. Dean's mailbox was full; Aaron's mailbox was full—that must be a sign, right? Maybe they were together. Or at least Aaron would know where Dean was. I got excited and started to dial Mom to tell her the good news: I had cracked the case, I'd found him. But then my brain started working again and I felt like a supreme idiot. Because Aaron's voice mail was probably just full because he never checked his messages; it probably had nothing to do with Dean. I hung up and lay back in the grass. I watched dark clouds pass over the sun and wondered who I should call next.

I called my mom next. She was a total mess. My parents had filed a missing person's report but it sounded like there wasn't too much the police could do besides "be on the lookout," whatever that meant. Plus Dean was eighteen and technically an adult, so he didn't get the AMBER alert played all over the TV and radio like a child would have. I tried to stay calm so my mom would calm down. I thought about telling her about the webcam stuff, but I didn't. I don't know why. It just didn't seem like it would help anything.

Throughout the day I ended up calling pretty much everyone in my phonebook who went to our school or knew Dean in some capacity. I even called Marla and Liz, who were not one bit of help, but at least answered their phones, so that was something. I realized that Dean didn't actually have that many friends. Most of the people I called were only acquaintances or knew him by reputation or had been to one of our parties. They didn't really *know* him. Maybe none of us did. I called Aaron about twelve more times and finally got him right before I went to bed.

"Aaron. It's Abby, Dean's sister."

"Oh. Hey. What's up?"

"Dean's been missing for almost two days. Do you have any idea where he is?"

"Uh, no. I haven't seen Dean in a while."

"Have you talked to him?"

"Nope. Not in a long time."

"Gotten any texts from him?"

"Uh-uh."

"Do you have any idea where he *might* be?"

"Not a clue."

"Did he ever talk about going away? On a trip or to visit . . . a friend?" I could hear straining noises in the background, like Aaron was trying to open something that was stuck.

"Uh, let's see . . . Ah! Got it!"

"What?"

"Oh, no, sorry . . . Just . . . got this jar lid off."

"Did he talk about going somewhere else?"

"Like, outside of Texas?"

"Yeah."

"Uh," Aaron said. "Hm, let me think."

More shuffling and weird noises came through the phone.

"Aaron?"

"Yeah?"

"Dean."

"Right, yeah. He talked about San Francisco sometimes."

"San Francisco?"

"Yeah. There was one time . . . I remember he said something like . . . he thought he could be happy there."

"Does he have any friends there? Does he know anyone there?"

"Not that I know of."

"Okay. Thanks, Aaron."

"So, he just took off? You guys haven't heard from him?"

"No. He hasn't called or texted anyone."

"Hm," Aaron said.

"Can you call me if you think of anything else? Or if he tries to get in touch with you? My parents are literally losing their minds."

"I will for sure."

"Thanks."

"Hey, Abby?"

"Yeah?"

"Um, could you text me? Like, once you hear from him or once he's back or whatever. Just so . . . you know . . ."

"Okay," I said. "I will."

"Cool. Okay. I'm sure he's okay."

"Yeah . . ."

"I gotta jet."

"Alright. Thanks, Aaron."

"See ya later. Good luck." He hung up.

It was not much, but it was something. It was the only real information anyone had given me all day that was possibly of any use. I wrote SAN FRANCISCO across my mirror in pink lipstick so I wouldn't forget in the morning. Then I fell into bed and had a fitful sleep full of dreams where I was drowning or else trying to save someone from drowning, or both.

I called Mom first thing the next morning and told her what Aaron had said about San Francisco.

"Okay," she said. "We'll let the police know."

"Alright."

"Thanks, Abby." She hung up.

I tried Dean's cell again. Same thing. If he would just check his stupid voice mail and there became room in the mailbox again, then at least I would know he was alive. But the mailbox was full, and it remained that way.

The next day was Wednesday, and it was a long day. I felt weaker than usual, nauseous, and Scott had to do laundry during his free period so we couldn't hang out. Jane and I played cards after we got back from the clinic, but I couldn't concentrate and lost every hand.

"Yo, Earth to Abby," she said. "Are you even here right now?"

"Sorry. I'm . . . having a hard time focusing."

"Yeah, I noticed. What's up with you, girl?"

I sighed. I told her about Dean disappearing and not being in contact with anyone for nearly four days.

"He'll come back," she said. "He's just out sowing his wild oats."

"I don't even know what that means," I said.

"Sowing your oats?"

"Yeah."

"Everyone's got wild oats to sow. You'll sow yours one day too."

"Okay. Whatever."

"Look, I'm sure he's fine. Try to relax. You're just at the start of your recovery. It's important that you minimize stress right now," Jane said, shuffling the deck.

"Easy for you to say! Your brother's not missing!"

"Okay. You gotta chill out." She set the pile of cards aside. "Why don't you go take a hot bath?"

"I don't have a bathtub." I began to cry. "I hate it here! I don't want to be here anymore, and I don't even have a bath-tub," I sobbed.

"Abby," Jane said softly, "none of us want to be here."

I looked into her dark eyes, shining with hurt. She was right, of course. "I'm sorry," I said, ashamed of myself.

She bit her lip, nodded.

My phone rang then. It was Mom. "I have to take this," I said. "I'll see you later, okay?"

"Yep." Jane turned away from me as I answered the phone. I left her apartment and went down the hall to mine.

"Mom? What's up?"

"I've booked you a ticket on the overnight bus. You're coming home tonight."

"Okay . . . ?"

"The police want to talk to you. We want to talk to you."

"Okay." My hands started to shake. She knew. I could tell from her voice.

"It leaves at 8:40 p.m."

"And you cleared it with Dr. Mike and everyone?"

"Yes," she said. "Family emergency."

"So . . . ?"

"Dad will pick you up in the morning. Try to get some sleep on the bus."

"Okay."

"See you tomorrow." She hung up.

The bus ride was terrible and seemed to last forever. I couldn't sleep. Obviously. Can anyone sleep on an overnight bus? As the hours ticked by, I felt worse and worse. My skin got hot and rashy. I felt weak and sick and gross. The bus stank like dirty diapers and I wanted to vomit for most of the ride.

I got into the station at six a.m. Dad was there, looking like he'd been on an overnight bus himself. He gave me a hug and took my bag.

"So what's going on?" I said when we were in the car, headed home.

He looked over at me then back to the road. He sighed. "We'll talk about it later. After you've had a rest and something to eat."

I closed my eyes. I was dizzy. When I opened them again we were in the driveway and Dad was opening my door. We went inside. He made me scrambled eggs and toast and juice and sat with me at the kitchen table while I ate. He gazed out the window. A crow hopped on the power line in front of our house. A garbage truck drove past.

"Where's Mom?"

"Sleeping. She was up most of the night."

I nodded. Pushed my plate away.

"Finished?"

"Yeah."

"Why don't you go up to your room and rest for a few hours? The police will be here at nine."

"Dad?" I said, my voice shaking.

"Yeah?"

"Can you tell me what all this is about?"

He looked down at the table and worried a spot in the wood with his thumbnail. "You remember James who I work with?"

"The computer whiz guy?"

"That's right."

"Yeah, I remember him."

"Well, we had James do some looking around on Dean's computer to see if we could get any insight into where he might be, and who he might be with."

"Oh."

My dad rubbed his eyes. They were red and watery.

I stared at him. I wanted to cry. I know he did too.

"Anyway," he said. "We can talk about this later. Go sleep for a bit."

"Okay." I went upstairs, took off my clothes and got into bed. I didn't think I'd be able to get to sleep but I was wrong.

When I woke up, Mom stood over my bed, watching me. It was a little freaky.

"Hi, Mom," I said, pulling up my covers.

"Get dressed and come downstairs please. The police are here."

"Okay."

She kept standing there for a moment. I looked around the room, toward the door. "Okay," she said, and left the room.

Two police officers stood in our living room. A man and a woman. They introduced themselves to me. Officer Santiago, that was the man, and Officer Boylan, the woman. I shook their hands and we all sat down. Dad brought everyone coffee, and after that, they pretty much got right to the point.

"We've come to understand that Dean was operating a webcam business out of this house," Officer Santiago said.

I looked at the carpet, feeling everyone's eyes on me.

"For the purpose of conducting sex acts in exchange for money," he continued.

Dad cleared his throat.

"Did you know about this, Abby?" Mom said.

I nodded, staring down at my hands.

"Why didn't you tell us? Why didn't you tell SOMEONE?" Mom screamed at me, her face scarlet. "YOU SHOULD HAVE TOLD US, ABBY! *You should have TOLD US!*"

Dad shushed her and pulled her close and she crumpled against his chest, convulsing with sobs, her throat hoarse from already crying so much.

The worst part was, I didn't know how to answer her. Maybe I never will.

"How long have you been aware of the existence of your brother's webcam business?" Officer Santiago said.

"Not long," I said. "A few weeks?"

"Do you know how long your brother has been conducting his business for?"

"No." I shook my head.

"TWO YEARS, ABBY!" my mom screamed at me. "OVER TWO YEARS! That means he was a *child* selling sex to adults. To . . . to pedophiles! *My* child." She broke down again, her body wracked with sobs.

"I didn't know," I whispered.

There are things I've done that I'm ashamed of. There are things I've done that I regret. But I knew not telling anyone about Dean was bigger than all of those things combined. And that if anything had happened to him, I would never forgive myself.

The police asked me more questions while Mom and Dad sat on the couch, glaring at me. Did I know any of the clients? Did I know the names or locations of any of the clients?

Did Dean talk about any of his clients in particular? Did he ever talk about meeting any of them in person? Did he get offers to meet them in person? Was I involved in the webcam business in any way? And more and more and more questions.

I answered all of them as best as I could, but really, I didn't know anything. I told them what Aaron had told me. That Dean thought he could be happy in San Francisco. Officer Boylan nodded and wrote in her notepad. They told us that they were going to seize Dean's hard drive and all of his computer equipment and turn it over to the FBI. The FBI would work on getting the transaction history from before Dean turned eighteen so they could try to build a case to prosecute all of his clients during that time.

"If or when Dean returns home," Officer Boylan said, "we're going to want him to testify against the clients he had as a minor."

"*When*," Mom said, gritting her teeth. "Not if."

Officer Boylan nodded once, and looked at Officer Santiago. Then Officer Santiago drilled me with another round of questions.

When they were finally done, I felt more exhausted than I ever had in my life. Dad walked them to the door. Mom stared at me, hard, while I pulled my legs up to my chest and tried not to fall apart.

"I'm sorry," I said.

She shook her head. Her eyes were puffy and bloodshot. She hated me. I could tell.

I felt cold and shaky and nauseous. My head hurt. Everything hurt.

"Go back to bed, Abby," she said. "You look like hell."

I got up again in the late afternoon. The three of us ordered a pizza and watched TV while we ate it. I could barely eat, I felt so weak. I knew they both hated me, and I didn't blame them. I had a bath, because I could, and went back to bed. I slept without dreaming and woke up in a cold sweat, shivering and blistering and wanting to die.

I didn't want to go back to Carville the next day, but I had to, because I'd had a reaction. A reaction happens because the drugs are killing all of the leprosy bacteria (which is a good thing) and your body is allergic to the dead bacteria floating around in your system. All your joints hurt so bad that it's painful to stand or walk or sit or even be in bed. You get massive headaches, your skin puffs up and you get more lesions and basically look and feel like a pile of crap. Nobody knows exactly what brings on reactions (not everyone gets them), but it probably has something to do with stress.

So Mom and Dad drove their leprous daughter back to

the clinic in Louisiana, not knowing if they had lost their only son. I curled up in the back seat because it hurt too much to sit up. We didn't talk, we didn't listen to music, we didn't eat sunflower seeds or M&M's. We just sat together in the car for seven hours, bearing the impossible weight of our sadness.

As soon as I got back, they started me on a new steroid treatment that was supposed to calm down the reaction. I slept for the rest of the day and all through the night and woke up Saturday, hoping with everything in me that while I'd been sleeping Dean had come home, or they had at least heard from him.

There was no news.

I got a muffin and juice from the kitchen then went for a little walk. Dr. Mike had told me that getting a bit of exercise would increase my circulation and help my body to heal faster. I was determined to walk for at least twenty minutes, even though I was super weak and exhausted. I found Scott, reading under a pecan tree by the lake.

"Hey, Tex!" He stood up when he saw me. He moved in to give me a hug.

"Better not," I said, backing away. "I'm really sore today."

"Oh," he said. "Okay." He shoved his hands in his pockets. "Where have you been? I missed you."

"My brother's still missing, and the police wanted to talk to me, so I went home."

"Oh no. Are you okay?"

"Not really."

"Sorry, stupid question."

"Yeah."

"How long has he been gone for now?"

"*Gone?* You make it sound like he's dead."

"That's not what I meant, Abby. Come on."

"Okay. Whatever." I took a deep breath. "I'm just . . . yeah. Today will be the sixth day."

"Oh, man. That's . . ."

"Yeah, look, I should go," I said as tears pricked my eyes.

"Do you have to? I was just going to take the rowboat out for a spin."

We both looked over at the old rowboat. It looked like a rickety hunk of junk.

"Good luck with that," I said.

"Thanks," he said. "Okay, well, I guess I'll see you at dinner then?"

"Okay." I turned away from him and walked back to my apartment as fast as I could. I wanted to be away from everyone in a dark cool room where I could breathe. And cry.

Why was Scott so nice to me anyway? It didn't make sense. Sometimes I wanted to scream at him, "GET AWAY FROM ME! I'M A LEPER!"

There had to be something seriously wrong with that guy for him to like me.

I tried to nap, but it was so uncomfortable to have my body touching the sheets that I couldn't stay in bed for very long. I took a long, hot shower and felt a little better. I wanted to do something but not with people around. I decided to visit the Carville library. I thought maybe I could find a really good book that could take my mind off everything, or at least help me relax a little bit. If that failed, I hoped they would at least have some old issues of *Cosmo* kicking around. Dr. Mike had said the same thing Jane had, that I needed to eliminate stress from my life, as much as possible, if I wanted my body to calm down and for the disease to go away. Which I did, obviously. But with Dean MIA (and quite possibly hacked up into little pieces inside someone's freezer) and the dead leprosy bugs floating around inside me, I was finding it difficult to eliminate stress from my life.

On my way to the library I saw Lester and Grace.

"Hello," Grace said. She didn't know who I was, only that someone was passing them in the long corridor.

"Hi, guys," I said.

Lester grinned. "That's our girl. Where you been, honey? You missed Mardi Gras!"

"Yeah," I said. "My brother's missing, so I had to go home."

"Oh, Lord." Lester's hand flew to his heart. "We are so sorry to hear that."

Grace shook her head. "That's terrible news, Abby."

"Yep," I said. "Pretty much."

"Listen," Grace said. "We were just on our way home to have some tea and cookies. Why don't you join us?"

"I really shouldn't. I have to—"

"Come on," Lester said. "They're chocolate chip, your favorite!"

"How did you know that's my favorite?"

"Because that's everybody's favorite!" Lester laughed.

"I don't know," I said. "I don't really feel like talking right now. No offense."

"Tell you what, you do the seeing, we'll do the talking," Lester said.

I smiled.

"Deal?"

"Okay, deal," I said.

I followed them to their little cottage. The hens and the turkey clucked around in the backyard. Lester and Grace said hello to the fowl and checked that they were all inside the fence, then we went inside. Grace made the tea and set a blue teapot on the table. Then she took a plate of cookies out of a cupboard and set that on the table. Lester brought over three teacups and saucers. All three had different flowers on them. He arranged each cup so that it matched the flowers on its saucer. I have no idea how he did that. Maybe it was a coincidence. Maybe there were tiny chips and bumps on each cup, like a Braille code, so that he would know which one matched which saucer. I didn't ask, because sometimes things like that are better left unknown.

We each had a cookie. The chocolate chunks were big and gooey and still warm.

"These are really good," I said.

"Grace made them special," Lester said.

"Oh. Is it a special occasion?"

"It's Saturday!" Grace said, then laughed.

"That's as good a reason as any, I guess," I said.

I took a sip of my tea. The flowers on my cup were magnolias, the state flower of Louisiana. I don't know why or how I knew that, but I did. I set the cup down and turned it in its saucer. It was strange being with Grace and Lester. People I would have never met, never talked to or even given a second glance. It was weird to think of all the events that had led up to me being in that moment with them, sitting at their kitchen table, starting with the church barbecue, nearly seven years ago. If a magnolia tree had been planted the day I ate the armadillo, it would only just be blooming for the first time.

"Abby?" Lester said. "Did you hear what Grace said?"

I looked up. "No." I coughed into my hand. "Sorry. What?"

"I had a brother who died, too," Grace said.

"My brother's not dead," I said. "He's missing."

"Oh. I'm sorry," she said, flustered. "I got mixed up."

"I mean, I guess he *could* be dead . . ." I swallowed my tea and choked on it a little. Saying it felt so wrong. Like it would somehow make it true. I knocked on the wooden table, wishing I hadn't said it out loud.

She nodded, slow. "It was a long time ago now, but, I still miss him . . ."

Lester reached out to touch her shoulder. She placed her hand on top of his and patted it.

"I had ten brothers and sisters," Grace said.

"Really?"

"Yes," she said. "I was the oldest girl. My brother, the one who died, was the only one older than me. He was one year older."

"Mine too," I said.

Grace nodded. "My mama died delivering the eleventh child, Cordelia, then after that it was up to me to look after everybody. Nine kids, a newborn, and my daddy too."

"Wow. That's . . ."

"It was a lot of work. I wanted to go to school, but I couldn't. Had too many kids to look after!"

Lester reached for another cookie and Grace slapped his hand away. Maybe she could see a little bit, I don't know. Maybe she felt his hand move.

"Oh, I did have some fun though. Had me a boyfriend. Sweet little thing."

Lester clucked his tongue and shook his head.

"We'd go out dancing in New Orleans, go to the picture shows, and we had a marvelous time together. He was studying to be a doctor."

Lester whistled through his teeth.

"So when I started getting the numbness in my hands, you know?"

"Yep," I said.

"Well, I told him about it, my boyfriend. I showed him this little pink spot that I had on my foot. We'd been dating over a year by this time, so I thought I could trust him, you know."

"Yeah," I said.

"And he said to me, 'I'm sure you're fine, sugar-beet. I'm sure you's just fine.' So I put my socks back on and I thought that was that."

"Right."

"Next day, wouldn't you know it, the Health Authority is knocking at my door. My boyfriend reported me to them. My own sweetheart turned me in."

"Good for nothing bum!" Lester said.

Grace gave him a gentle smile. "So they told my daddy I have to go to Carville and does he want to take me or should they?"

I took a drink of my tea, nodding pointlessly.

"So, he borrowed our neighbor's car and drove me up here hisself the next morning."

"That's rough," I said.

"Oh, it was sad. I had to say goodbye to all them kids. I *raised* those kids. And I didn't see any of them again. Not until my brother's funeral five years later. They didn't even write to tell me he had passed. Had to read about it in the paper. I saw it in the obituaries. He'd been killed in a car accident, and I said, that's my brother. I'm going to pay my last respects. So I went through the hole in the fence, because we weren't allowed out in those days, not even if our own kin had passed away. I found a ride back to New Orleans and went straight to the church. Well, I found out at my brother's funeral that my family had told everyone I had died! Didn't they get some surprise when I walked into the church in my Sunday best, alive and well!"

We all laughed.

"Even some of my little brothers and sisters who were too young to remember thought I was dead, because that was the story they'd been told. I said, no wonder I've never gotten any letters from any of my old friends or my aunties or cousins, they all think I'm dead!" She chuckled, shook her head, then sipped from her teacup. "That broke my heart, though. Broke it wide open." She sighed deeply. "I paid my respects to my brother and I said goodbye to my family and came back to Carville. When I got back, everybody said, 'How was your trip home?' And I said, 'This is my home now.'"

"Mmhm," Lester said.

"And that was that. I never saw anyone from my family ever again."

"That's so sad," I said.

"Yes, it is," said Grace. "But no one ever promised there wouldn't be sadness in this life."

Lester reached his hand across the table until it found Grace's. They smiled at each other. Somehow, they each knew that the other one was smiling.

"I've been very blessed though," Grace said. "Even though I've had this disease, I've been very lucky. I've met all kinds of wonderful people. People that I would have never met if I didn't get this disease."

"Like me!" Lester said.

"That's right, lemon-drop," Grace said, turning her face toward him. "And Abby." She smiled in my general direction.

I sat with them a while longer. We all had another cookie and another cup of tea.

"When they found out I had the gazeek," Lester said, "my mama sent me away the very same day."

"The gazeek?"

"It's another name for the disease," Grace said, nodding.

"Oh," I said. "Huh."

"I was ten years old," Lester said, cradling his gibbled hands one inside the other. "Mama said, 'I might not see you again, but I want you to know that you're a good boy. You didn't do nothing wrong. And I'll always love you no matter what. Even if we're not together anymore.' She gave me a hug and a kiss, then the police put chains around my hands and feet and put me in the back of an old horse trailer and hauled me up here. That was it. I never did see Mama again. Or my daddy. Or any of my five brothers and sisters. My daddy owned a store, see? So if the town had found out I had the disease, the store would've gone bankrupt. My family would've starved." He coughed, then cleared his throat. "I can see the sense in it now, but it sure did sting at the time. *Wooowee!*"

"How long have you been here?" I said.

"Eighty-one years this May," Lester said.

"Seventy-four years," Grace said.

"Holy sh—"

"Mmhm. Some people do say this place is holy," Lester said.

"The nuns certainly used to think so," said Grace.

"I thought that getting this disease, the . . . gazeek?" I said.

"Mmhm," Lester said, grinning.

"I thought that it was the worst thing that could ever happen to me," I said. "But, it wasn't."

Grace and Lester waited expectantly.

"Dean disappearing was."

They nodded.

"I don't know where he is or if he's even alive." I began to cry. I couldn't help it. "If I could just be certain that he was alive, then I feel like it would be okay. I wouldn't even need to know where he is but . . . I don't know." I pressed my palms into my eyes. "I'm sorry, I . . ."

"That's alright, honey," Grace said. "You don't need to apologize for anything."

Lester pulled a white handkerchief from his pocket and handed it to me. I blew my nose into it, hard.

What if Dean was dead? It would be my fault. I should've told someone about the webcam stuff. I should've known. But he couldn't die. He couldn't. He was my brother. Nobody knew me like Dean did. No one ever would.

Grace reached for my hand and squeezed it, placing her other gnarled palm on top and patting my hand gently. "It's a very hard life, Abby," she said. "All we can do is get through it the best way we know how."

"Yeah," I said, blowing my nose again.

"You should go rest now, Abby. We've talked your ear off for long enough," Lester said. "People lose ears all the time around here."

We laughed. I wiped my tears with the handkerchief and then held it out to give it back to Lester. He didn't see it, of course. "Um, what should I do with this?"

"Keep it," he said. "Might bring you luck." He grinned.

"Okay. Um, thanks." That was the first time I had ever used a handkerchief. Normally stuff like that grossed me out. But after you get a disease like leprosy, I guess your gross-tolerance significantly increases. I thanked them and walked back to my apartment. I took small steps and deep breaths, and even though I hurt all over, I felt a tiny bit better than I had before. I got into bed and lay awake thinking about Grace's story. About how it would feel to be considered dead when you were still alive. I decided I wouldn't let that happen to Dean. No matter how long he was missing for, no matter how much time passed without hearing from him, until we had indisputable evidence, I would never consider him to be dead. I wouldn't let other people talk about him that way either. For now, he was just . . . somewhere else. He had to be.

The next day was Sunday. It had been a week since the last time I'd seen Dean. I slept through breakfast, got up, showered, then walked around in a daze, thinking dark thoughts. For *years* Dean had been doing this webcam shit. But no one had any idea. How had none of us known? And *what else* didn't we know?

I called his phone a couple of dozen times, just in case. Nothing. I felt weak and sick and awful but I tried to walk around as much as I could. I stared out toward the lake; the sunlight sparkled on the water. A beautiful boy with shaggy brown hair sat under a pecan tree, reading. My heart sped up as I walked toward him.

My shadow fell over him, and he squinted up at me and grinned. "Hey, Tex."

"Hey, Okie." I glanced down at his book. The cover was blue with an image of a bird on it. "What are you reading?"

"Oh, it's . . . well, you might have heard of it. *Jonathan Livingston Seagull*?"

I shook my head. "What's it about?"

"It's about a seagull."

I half-laughed.

"He's an outcast because he wants to fly . . ."

"Uh-huh."

"I don't know. It's about more than that, but it's kind of hard to explain right now. I'm only partway through. It's pretty cool so far. I think you'd like it."

"Sounds like it's for the birds."

Scott laughed. "Yeah, maybe." He smiled at me, his pale green eyes crinkling at the edges. "Any word on your brother?"

"No, nothing." I checked my phone. "Yep. Still nothing."

He patted the grass beside him for me to sit down. I sat next to him with my knees bent and rested my forehead on my knees. "I don't really want to talk about it right now if that's okay."

"Sure." He rubbed my shoulder gently. I flinched and leaned away. He sighed.

"I don't get this," I said.

"Get what?"

"This. What is this?" I gestured to his arm. My shoulder. The two of us.

He shrugged. "I like you, Abby."

"But, I mean, *why*?"

"Why?" he laughed.

"Yeah. Why? Look at me; I'm hideous. I'm in a leprosy treatment center for fuck's sake. What is there to like about that?"

He stared out at the lake.

I followed his gaze. "I used to be pretty," I whispered. "But not anymore. Now I'm a monster."

"You're not a monster."

"I feel like a monster. I feel so disgusting, Scott, I don't even know how you can stand to look at me." I buried my face in my arms.

"Hey, hey . . . Come on now."

"I can't," I said, still hiding my face from him.

"Listen," he said. "What's the most important thing you've ever done? The thing you're the most proud of?"

"I don't know." I rubbed my eyes against my forearms.

"Come on, think about it."

"I'm not proud of anything I've done. I've led a vain and shallow existence."

"I don't believe that," he said.

"Well, you should. It's the truth."

"What's the most important thing, then? The thing that if you hadn't done it, the whole world would be different?"

"I'm not . . . I don't . . ."

"*C'mon*, Abby."

I looked up at him. "I saved my brother's life once."

"You see!"

"He had alcohol poisoning. Stopped breathing. Heart stopped. Everything. I gave him CPR. I cracked a few of his ribs, but the paramedics said I saved his life."

"You see, that's what I'm talking about."

"What are you talking about?"

"*You.*"

"What do you mean?"

"That was *you*, Abby. It had nothing to do with the way you look or your hair or clothes or anything like that."

"My clothes? What's wrong with my clothes?"

"Nothing! Nothing's wrong with your clothes, okay? Will you please just listen to me?"

"Okay . . ."

"When I say I like you, that's the you I mean. The you that saved your brother. The you that comes from there. That place." He tapped on his chest, over his heart.

"Oh."

"Do you . . . ? Do you like me?"

I looked at him from the corner of my eye. Then buried my head in my arms again. "Yes! A lot!"

He laughed. "Well, okay then. That's settled."

"I just don't know what the point is though. I mean, you're leaving soon. We'll probably never see each other again."

"I don't see why we wouldn't."

I looked up at him. "Really?"

"There are roads that connect Texas and Oklahoma, aren't there?"

"Yeah."

"So, then, it won't be that hard."

"But seriously though? Because I don't want to say that we're going to see each other again and then not actually do it. If we're not going to, then I'd rather just say we're not going to and be done with it."

"I, Scott Avery, will do everything in my power to see you, Abby . . . What's your last name?"

"Furlowe."

"I, Scott Avery, will do everything in my power to see you, Abby Furlowe, again after we leave this place known as Carville, Louisiana, located in the United States of America."

I giggled.

"Okay?"

"Okay," I said, nodding. "I'd like that."

"Good. Me too." He smiled at me.

I wanted to kiss him, but I couldn't. Not when my face was all puffy and I had sores on my neck. When I was better, when the disease was gone and my face had cleared, then I would kiss him. And it would be great. Even though it might be a long time coming, I believed him when he said we would see each other again. I don't know why, but I believed him.

"What are you doing now?" Scott asked.

I covered a big yawn. "I guess I should go back to my

room and have a nap," I said. "I'm supposed to try to get as much rest as possible."

"Okay. I'll walk you back." He stood up and extended his hand to help me up.

When I reached to grab his hand he pulled it back and ran it through his hair. "Psych!" He laughed. "No, just kidding. Here." He reached his hand down again. I grabbed for it and he reached around in his back pocket to check his phone. He laughed silently while he swiped the screen. "Okay, okay, for real this time." He put his phone away and gave me his hand. I took it and stood up.

"Jerk." I punched him lightly on the shoulder. I laughed and so did he.

We walked awhile without saying anything. The sun felt warm on the back of my neck.

"It will be nice," I said, looking up at him.

"What will?"

"Seeing you. Outside of here. It will be good."

"Yeah," he said. "It will be." He glanced at me, then reached for my hand. We held hands all the way back to my apartment. "Well, I guess I'll see you later," he said, not letting go of my hand.

"Okay," I said.

"Are you accepting hugs today?"

I nodded and he hugged me as if I were made of glass and he was afraid to break me. "Have a good nap," he said into my ear, still holding me against him.

"Thanks." I began to pull away but he didn't let me go. After a moment he did.

"Okay," he said. "See you soon."

"Bye."

I climbed the stairs to my apartment, feeling his eyes on me. I glanced back and he still stood there, looking up at me. He gave me a goofy wave. *That kid is so weird*, I thought. And yet . . . and yet . . .

I went into my room and set my alarm for dinner. I undressed and got into bed. I lay awake for a while thinking about Scott. I wondered if I would love him. If I were falling in love with him. My stomach did a series of roller-coaster loops. Maybe. I wished that I had saved my virginity for someone I actually cared about. Someone who cared for me. For anyone other than Chad Bennett. I ran my hand along the edge of my panties. Maybe I could be one of those born-again virgins. Not the surgery, but just, like, reclaiming my virginity until someone worthy came along, or until I got married. Or at least until I turned eighteen. Whichever came first. I rolled over and laughed into my pillow. Right, Abby.

Soon, I fell into a feverish sleep. I dreamt I could see all the way down inside myself. And I was not beautiful.

After dinner that night, Jane came back to my room with a tub of rocky road ice cream she had pilfered from the staff kitchen. We sat on my bed eating it and flipping through old copies of *Vanity Fair*.

"You would look so fly in this dress," she said, showing me a photo of a black-and-yellow cut-out dress.

"You think?" I said. "Those are our school colors."

"Well, it wouldn't have to be those colors. Just the style I think would really suit your body type."

"Cool. Yeah. I like it. I don't have anything like that."

She took the magazine back, looking pleased with herself.

"Oh, hey, I forgot to tell you, you would look really great with purple hair."

She laughed. "What?"

"Yeah, I had this dream. It was weird, I won't bore you with the details, but you were in it, you had purple hair and it looked really good on you."

"Huh," she said. She threw the magazine on the bed and got up to examine herself in the mirror. She touched her hair, her face, moved her head from side to side. "Yeah, maybe."

"Totally," I said.

"Oh, that reminds me," Jane said. "I saved you this." She pulled a large gold coin out of her pocket and tossed it to me.

I grabbed it out of the air. "What is it?"

"It's a Carville doubloon. They're minted here and they throw them out at the Mardi Gras parade." She pouted at me. "It's really too bad you missed Mardi Gras, Abby. It's only, like, the funnest night of the whole entire year."

"Yeah, I had some other stuff going on."

"I know. Maybe next time," she said. "You'd love it. I promise."

I was hoping there wouldn't be a next time. I turned the coin over in my hand. "There's an armadillo on it."

"Yeah. It's the mascot here."

"Why?"

"Because they used armadillos for testing, and that's how they discovered that the sulfone drugs worked. So the armadillo's like a symbol of hope. You know, that the disease can be cured."

"But it's also the reason some of us are here . . ."

"Well," Jane said, shrugging. "It's a two-sided coin."

"Huh." I flipped it over. It was the same on the other side. "Thanks." I set it on my nightstand.

"Listen," Jane said, "I wasn't going to tell you this because I didn't want you to be mad at me."

"What is it?"

"Promise you won't be mad."

"I don't know. Tell me first, and then I'll tell you if I'm mad or not."

She took a deep breath. "I'm leaving tomorrow. I'm going back to New York."

"*Tomorrow?*" My eyes began to well up. "*And you weren't even going to tell me?*"

"See. You're mad."

"I'm not mad. I'm . . . just . . ." I shook my head, fanning my face. I couldn't stop the tears from coming.

Jane sat down on the bed beside me and gave me a hug. "Oh! Don't cry! Okay, you can cry if you want. But don't get any snot on my blouse. It's dry clean only."

I half-laughed, half-cried as she hugged me and rocked me. I hadn't realized it until she'd said she was leaving, but Jane was my best friend.

"You can't leave tomorrow," I said.

"Why not? Did we have plans tomorrow?"

"No. It's just . . . it's too soon."

"I've been here six weeks, Abby. I'm ready to get back to my life."

"But—"

"Things to see. People to do." She clicked her tongue twice, gave me a wink.

"But, I need you here. What am I going to do without you?" I said.

She shrugged. "Play checkers with Barry?"

We laughed.

"He's actually pretty good," she said.

I cried harder.

"Oh, honey, you'll be fine."

"No. I won't be."

"We can write! You write to me first and I'll write you back. Promise. It'll be fun. It'll be like in the olden days when people actually wrote letters to each other."

I sniffled. "Okay," I said, wiping my nose on the back of my hand.

"Yeah?" She handed me a tissue.

"Yeah." I nodded. "Okay." I blew my nose.

"Cool."

I smiled at her through my tears. She gave me another hug and smoothed my hair. "You're going to be alright," Jane said. "Everything is going to be alright."

It was hard to believe, but I wanted so badly for her to be right.

Saying goodbye to Jane the next morning was really hard. I wanted her to go back to her life in New York and have fun and eat cheesecake, but I also wanted her to stay at Carville and be my friend. I was pretty lacking in the friend department, and I was going to miss her.

As Jane waved to me through the window of her taxi, I got the feeling that it wouldn't be the last time I saw her. Maybe I'd visit her in New York. Maybe she'd visit me in California, or wherever the hell I ended up. There are people who come into your life for a reason, a season or a lifetime, or whatever bullshit Jane would say. I guess she was one of those people. I just didn't know which one yet. She blew me a kiss and I caught it and tucked it away in my back pocket for safekeeping. Whatever little bits of my heart Marla and Liz had left intact broke away then, as Jane's taxi blew up dust clouds along the only road out of town.

I stayed in the parking lot after her taxi was gone, kicking rocks and feeling sorry for myself, wondering if I'd ever hear her laugh again and trying not to cry. After a few minutes, this little purple truck pulled in, blasting hard techno. Pink fuzzy dice dangled from the rearview mirror. Two young guys got out and slammed their doors shut. One of them was slender and blond and the other one . . . the other one was Dean.

My knees buckled as I gaped at him. He had dyed the tips of his hair hot pink and pierced both of his ears. I think he was wearing eyeliner. He was grinning as he walked toward me, arms spread wide.

"Hey, sis," he said, as he folded me into a hug.

"You asshole." I sobbed into his neck. "*You fucking asshole.*"

"Nice to see you too." He stepped back.

I glanced at the other guy.

"This is Kyle," Dean said. "Kyle, Abby."

"Hi." Kyle shook my hand, smiling. He wore a rhinestone pinkie ring. "I love your hair," he said. "It's *so* pretty."

"Kyle's a photographer," Dean said.

I touched my hair. Jane had braided it for me the night before and I'd slept on it wet so it was all wavy and volumized. "Thanks," I said.

"You're welcome!"

I turned back to Dean. "Why didn't you call? Or text someone? Do you know how worried we've all been? You're a *missing person*, Dean. Police are looking for you. Mom and Dad—"

"My phone was stolen," he said.

"And, so what? There are no other phones on planet Earth you could've used?" I gestured at Kyle. "*He* doesn't have a phone you could've borrowed?"

"Look, Abby. I needed some time, okay."

"Time for what? Time to make us think you had been kidnapped? Tortured? Murdered? Because that's what we thought, Dean. I thought I was never going to see you again."

Kyle gave me a sad pouty face and looked over at Dean.

Dean sighed. "I'm sorry, Abby. I didn't mean to . . . I just . . . I really needed some time to figure things out. Time where I didn't talk to anyone from home."

"But you could've just texted! Just texted or emailed to let us know you were alright!" I yelled at him.

"I know. I'm sorry. I was selfish," he said.

"Pfff, that's the understatement of the year," I said.

"Look, do you have anything to drink? We've been driving for hours and we're really thirsty."

I sighed and spun around, leading them back to my apartment.

I got them some water and they sat at the little table and I sat on the bed, staring at them.

"I don't think I'm ever going to be able to forgive you for this," I said.

"Okay," Dean said. Like it didn't really matter one way or the other.

"Have you seen Mom and Dad yet?" I said.

Dean shook his head. "I wanted to see you first."

"So they don't know you're alive?"

Dean shrugged.

I pulled out my phone.

"Just wait," he said.

"What? I have to tell them."

"Just wait a little while. We're heading there after this anyway."

I set my phone down beside me. "They know everything, Dean. The FBI seized your hard drive. You're in some serious shit."

He nodded slowly, scratching his thumbnail against a groove in the table.

I eyed Kyle. "Is he . . . ? Is this . . . ? Who is he?"

Kyle grinned at me. "Ever heard of the Kyle High Club?"

"Uh, no."

"It's kind of a long story," Dean said.

"Look where we are," I said, glancing around the room. "Do you think I'm going anywhere soon?"

"Okay, well. Thing is . . ." Dean fiddled with the rim of his water glass.

"Just tell her," Kyle said.

Dean shrugged. "Kyle and I are both webcam boys," Dean said.

"*Were*," Kyle said, touching Dean's hand.

"Right. *Were*."

"Okay . . ." I said.

"We both got into it around the same time," Dean said.

"And we were *always* in competition!" Kyle said. "We were always trash-talking each other to steal customers."

Dean blushed. "Yeah, so, we ended up having a lot of the same clients, and we'd chat about which ones were good and which ones to block and, you know, basically helped each other figure stuff out."

"And then . . . ?" Kyle said.

"And then, Kyle had the idea that we should join forces. Like, create a joint site so that we could maximize our profits."

Kyle nodded. "What can I say? I'm an upwardly mobile twink!"

Dean gazed at him, puppy-dog eyed. "But I told him if we were actually going to do it, I wanted to meet in person, so I could tell if he was legit or not and see if we'd actually be able to work together," Dean said.

"Turns out, we work *very well* together." Kyle winked at me.

"Uh-huh," I said. "So, *where* have you been all this time?"

"Have you ever heard of the Castro?" Dean said.

"No," I said.

Kyle gasped.

"You mean, like, Fidel Castro?"

"Oh, honey," Kyle said. "You haven't lived."

I glared at him.

"The Castro is this neighborhood in San Francisco," Dean said.

I nodded. So Aaron had been right.

"It's a magical place," Kyle said.

I raised my eyebrows at him.

"There's just so much history there. It's really, really a special place. An *important* place."

"It was one of the first gay neighborhoods in the U.S.," Dean said.

"And it fucking *rocks*," said Kyle.

They grinned at each other. "Kyle has an apartment there," Dean said.

"I see."

"So, long story short, I helped your brother come out of the closet this week, and he helped me realize that I don't want to be a web-whore anymore."

"I'm quitting too," Dean said. "It was good money while it lasted, but I'm over it."

"Plus, I'd be way too jealous," Kyle said.

They both laughed.

"So you weren't kidnapped and locked in a basement. You were never hurt by anyone," I said.

"No," Dean said. "I was figuring out my life."

"So . . . what now?"

"Now, we're going to see Mom and Dad."

"He's going to come out to your parents," Kyle said, squeezing Dean's hand.

"Yep," Dean said, taking a deep breath, nodding. "Then, we're going to pack up all my stuff and drive back to California and . . . I'm moving in with Kyle."

Kyle's face looked like a jack-o'-lantern, he was smiling so big.

"Whoa. What? You're moving to San Francisco?"

He nodded, looking happier than I'd ever seen him.

"What about graduating from high school?"

"I can finish over there. All I have to do is write my finals anyway."

"What about . . . your life?"

"My life sucked." He shrugged. "I'm getting a new one."

"So . . . ?"

"So, I wanted to come say goodbye to you before I left."

"Oh." I looked down at my hands.

"Don't look so sad. You've wanted me gone for years."

"Not really though," I said in a small voice. "Not that far away."

"You can come visit anytime," Dean said. "There's even a pull-out couch for you to sleep on."

"Oh, my friends will *adore* you! You *have* to come," Kyle said. "Please? Please? Please?"

"Okay," I said.

"Yay!" He clapped his hands.

Dean smiled. The three of us sat quiet for a moment. Kyle and Dean gazed at each other, their eyes shining.

"Well," I said, "I'm just glad you're alright. I was . . . it was really scary, okay? You don't even know."

Dean nodded. "I know it was a jerk move," he said. "Not calling."

"Total jerk move."

He nodded again.

"You aged Mom ten years. At least ten. Maybe twenty."

"Shit."

"Dad didn't really care though. He always liked me best anyway."

"Shut up." He play-punched me in the shoulder.

I laughed.

"Well." Dean cleared his throat. "I guess we'd better get going. We want to make it to Texas tonight."

"Ooh! I'm so excited to see Texas," Kyle said. "I've never been."

"Huh," I said.

"Is it true that everything's bigger in Texas?" he asked Dean.

Dean's face flushed as he laughed, shaking his head.

"I guess I'll find out soon enough," Kyle said.

Dean stood up and tucked in his chair, so did Kyle.

"I'll walk you back," I said, standing.

"It's okay, you don't have to," Dean said.

"I want to."

He nodded and we all headed out the door and down the stairs.

On the way back to the parking lot, Kyle and Dean held hands. I walked along beside them, and for the first time in ages, felt something like peace.

"Dean?" I said, as we approached the shiny purple truck.

"Yeah?"

"I'm happy for you," I said. "I really am. For both of you."

"Thanks, Abs."

Kyle flashed me a megawatt smile. Even his teeth were shiny. "It was *so* great to meet you!" He hugged me and kissed me on both cheeks. "And you are welcome to come visit us anytime! Come sooner than later!" He got in the truck and started it up, then fiddled with the stereo.

I stared at Dean. "He just kissed me," I said.

"Yup."

"But . . . does he know what this is? Why I'm in here?"

"Yup."

"What the—?"

Dean shrugged. "That's just Kyle."

"He's . . ."

"Yup." Dean laughed, then hugged me. "Bye, Abby."

"Hey, thanks for coming up here. I . . . it really means a lot to me that you came."

He nodded and opened the passenger door of the truck.

"Bye, Dean."

"See ya later, sister."

I waved as they pulled out of the parking lot. Kyle honked the horn and they both waved to me, techno music blasting the bass of a heartbeat.

On the way back to my apartment I texted my mom: Dean's okay. He's on his way to see you. Just left here. New friend in tow.

She replied right away: Thank God!!! Who's this friend?

I typed: His name is Kyle.

I touched my cheek where Kyle had kissed me, then added: I think you'll like him.

I slept well that night for the first time since Dean had left home. I didn't have any nightmares. I didn't have any night sweats. When my alarm went off in the morning, I could actually get out of bed. I felt a sharp icicle stab into the center of my chest when I remembered that Jane was gone. And then ten more icicles pierced me when I realized that she would be gone tomorrow, and the next day, and every day after that. But I didn't cry. I hurried to get ready and hustled to breakfast so that I would have time to catch the bus to the clinic in Baton Rouge. I wanted to talk to Dr. Rodriguez. I knew I had to talk to somebody, because I had a lot of feelings swimming around inside me that I didn't know how to sort out or what to do with, and I didn't want to keep them all inside. It felt like they could boil over and explode at any moment. I'm not sure what that would look like, but I knew it would be messy.

We sat in Dr. Rodriguez's new office. It was much bigger and painted sky blue, and the sun shone through the blinds, making all the dust particles in the air sparkle.

"I like your new office," I said.

"Me too," she said.

"The posters are gone."

"Yes," she said.

"That's good," I said.

"Why is that good?"

"I hated the posters."

She folded her hands together and studied me. "Hate is a very strong word, Abby."

"Well, I strongly disliked the posters," I said. "Maybe even hated them. Let me think. Yep, I hated them."

"Any particular reason the posters elicited such strong emotions from you?"

I picked at my nails for a while.

"Abby?"

"I found them insulting," I said, looking up at her. "Like they were rubbing it in my face."

"Rubbing what in your face?"

"With the figure skating and the mountain climbing."

She looked at me, her mouth a tight, thin line.

"Because I won't be able to do any of those things anymore. I won't be able to 'reach for the stars' or 'live my dreams' or any of that crap."

"Because of your injuries?"

"I can't even cheer anymore," I said. "I'm basically an invalid."

"I'd say that's a bit of an exaggeration."

"That's easy for you to say! You're not the one who—"

She crinkled her face at me. Her eyebrows knit together into one perfect fuzzy unit.

"Oh forget it," I said. "Never mind."

"I'm here to help you, Abby. What can we talk about today that would best help you? Is it the posters? It can be anything you want. You can say anything you want in here. You don't need to censor yourself. I'm not going to get angry with you. Okay?"

"Okay."

"So . . . ?"

"What I really want to know is, *why*?"

"Why?"

"Why did this happen to me?"

She sighed. "Abby, for some questions, there are no answers."

I rubbed my eyes and held my head in my hands. Suddenly, it was too heavy to hold up.

"How are you feeling these days?" she asked.

"I . . . I have a lot of feelings."

She nodded. "That's perfectly normal."

I raised my head. "Yeah, but . . . I want to get them out," I said, pushing my palms away from me.

Dr. Rodriguez gave me a small smile. She suggested that I start writing. I could write anything I wanted, my life story, whatever. "Many patients find it very therapeutic to write about their experience with Hansen's disease," she said. "Some of them have even gone on to publish their books."

"Really?"

"Yes, their books are all in the library here. You can check them out."

"Do I need a card or . . . ?"

"No. We just ask that you return the books once you've finished with them."

"Cool."

"And don't read in the bathtub."

I laughed. "That shouldn't be a problem since I don't have a bathtub."

"Don't read in the lake either."

"Do people actually swim in that lake?"

"Some do, yes."

"What about alligators?"

"They've been known to swim in there also."

"Isn't that, like . . . super dangerous?"

"Yes."

"I guess people gotta get their kicks somehow."

"Indeed." She opened her desk drawer and pulled out a red spiral notebook. "I'll give you this to get started," she said, handing it to me.

"Thanks."

She smiled.

I gazed down at the shiny new notebook. "Maybe I'll write a book, and it'll get published, and someone will want to turn it into a movie, and they'll ask me to play myself in the movie."

"Maybe," Dr. Rodriguez said.

"That would be awesome."

"It certainly would be," she said.

I started writing my book that day and it felt really good to get it all out in words, to see them all there on the lined pages in front of me, so I kept working on it. Even though what had happened to me didn't make any sense, and I knew there was no real reason for any of it, at least I could put it into sentences and paragraphs that made sense on the page. It was something I could do. Something I had control over. When I filled up the first notebook, I asked Dr. Rodriguez for another one. She pulled her desk drawer open and handed me a new notebook. Same as the last. She didn't say anything, just smiled at me as if to say, *See? I told you so.*

Scott and I were spending a lot of time together, neither one of us talking about the fact that he was leaving at the end of the week. Mostly we hung out by the lake because it was cooler down there and no one was around to bother us. He would read and I'd write in my notebook. One day he asked me to read him what I'd written.

"No," I said. "I can't."

"Why not?"

"I don't know why," I said. "I just can't."

"I won't laugh."

I looked down at my notebook. The pages fluttered in the breeze.

"Unless it's funny," he said. "Then I might laugh."

"It's not funny," I said. "It's tragic."

"Perfect," he said. "I love tragedies."

"I don't know," I said.

"Come on!" He tossed his book aside.

"I don't know, Scott. What if—"

"What do I have to do? Get down on my knees and beg?"

I looked up. There was a magnolia tree above us, bursting with pink and white flowers. It was so pretty. It smelled like almonds and vanilla. I looked back at Scott.

He was down on one knee, his hands clasped together. "Please?!"

"*Okay.* Fine." I laughed.

"Yes! Finally!"

"From the beginning?"

"Wherever you want."

I flipped back to the first page of my notebook and began to read to him: "They think I got it from an armadillo."

He lay back in the grass, folded his hands behind his head and gazed up at the sky. Magnolia petals drifted down around us as I read. At one point, Scott reached up and gently plucked out a petal that had landed in my hair. I looked down at him and smiled. He smiled back.

"Keep going," he said. "Don't stop."

I read to him until the dinner bell rang. Then we walked to the mess hall together holding hands.

"That was really good, Abby. You're a good writer."

"You're just saying that," I said.

"No way. I wouldn't just say that."

"Okay. Well, thanks, I guess."

"Maybe if the acting thing doesn't work out, you could be a writer."

"You think?"

"You could probably get that published, what you're writing now. It's a really interesting story."

"It's not a story," I said. "It's my life. It's what happened."

He grinned. "Even better."

Eventually the day came, Scott's last day of the Youth Challenge Program. I woke up with a lead weight inside my chest, knowing he was leaving before sunrise the next morning. He had a lot of cadet crap to do that day, closing ceremonies and packing and whatever, so I didn't see him for more than fifteen minutes all day. It sucked. At dinner he came up behind me in line.

"Hey," he said, touching my shoulder.

I turned around. "Oh. Hey."

He leaned toward me. "Leave your door unlocked tonight," he said in a half-whisper.

"Okay," I said, feeling a hot blush rise into my face.

"Okay." He smiled. "I have to go now. But I'll see you later."

I nodded.

That night, Scott snuck out of his barracks and came to my apartment. That's what I loved most about Scott; he wasn't afraid of anything.

"Hey." He stood just inside my door, silhouetted in the low light.

"Hey," I said. I rubbed my eyes, looked at my phone. It was after one in the morning. I lifted the bedcovers and shifted over to make room for him. He slid down his jeans and pulled off his shirt and got into bed beside me. He rolled on his side to face me.

"Hey," he said. His eyes shone in the dark.

"Hey."

"Hey," he said, softly, looking at my lips.

"Hey," I whispered.

We kissed. Then we kissed some more. No one had ever kissed me like that before. I can't say exactly how it was different. There was . . . feeling behind it. It was more than just kissing. It was . . . communicating. At the risk of sounding super cheesy, it was . . . magical.

He ran his hands down the length of my body. I liked it, but I was still sore, and I guess he could tell I was uncomfortable. He pulled his face away from mine. "Are you okay?"

"Yeah. It's not you . . . it's me."

He laughed.

"No, but for real though."

"What's the matter?"

I moaned and flopped on my back. "I still feel so gross."

"You're not gross, Abby. I promise you. You're not." He kissed me on the cheek.

"Thanks," I whispered. I could feel tears collecting at the corners of my eyes.

"Can I just hold you?"

I nodded.

"Roll over."

So I did. He slipped his arms around me and held me close. I could feel his warmth envelop me. It was the nicest thing I've felt.

"Is this okay?" he said.

"Yes," I said. "This is very okay."

He closed his hand around mine. "Good."

We stayed like that for a while until I was almost asleep. Then Scott said, "Okay, my turn." And he flipped onto his other side so that I could spoon him.

I curled my body around his and put my hand on his chest. I could feel his heart beating. It was strong and steady and sounded reassuring. I let out a sigh.

"What is it?" he said.

"Nothing. It's just . . ."

"What?"

"I was just hoping that this isn't the last time we'll get to do this."

"It won't be," he said.

I could hear him smile in the dark.

When I opened my eyes to the bright light of day, he was gone. His dog-eared copy of *Jonathan Livingston Seagull* lay on the pillow beside me.

I turned toward the wall, fighting the wave of misery that threatened to crash over me. I reached for the book. He had written his phone number inside the front cover, an *x* and his name below. I pressed the book to my chest and stared up at the ceiling, wondering if it was too soon to call him.

I had to stay at Carville for another month to get my body calmed down from the reaction and make sure everything was back on track. Since Jane and Scott were gone, I ended up writing a lot. I filled three more red notebooks and still had more to say about what it felt like to be a real, live leper. I spent a lot of time in the library. I learned a ton about the other people who had lived (and died) at Carville. Their stories were so, so sad, but reading them made me feel less alone. I was like them; they were like me. I was just lucky to be born when I was, when there was a drug treatment that killed the bacteria. I wouldn't have to have any limbs amputated, I wouldn't die as a result of the disease and my family wouldn't tell people that I had died because they were so ashamed of me. Reading their stories made me feel like I was part of something, and it was something that had been going on for a long, long time. They were brave, all of them. And maybe I was too.

One of the autobiographies I read was by a man named Stanley Stein. He was a pharmacist who started a newspaper from Carville and advocated for the rights of the patients. He was the person who started the movement to change the name of the disease to Hansen's disease and to stop using the word *leper*. There was this one quote in his book that I copied out and taped to my mirror so that I would see it every day. It said:

> It is not what we have lost that matters most,
> but what we choose to do with what we have left.

It made sense to me, and I decided to believe in it. Like, instead of getting depressed that I couldn't cheer anymore and wouldn't get the scholarship and wouldn't be able to go to USC for acting, I could get serious about my writing and try to keep getting better at that, and maybe someday someone would want to publish something I had written. It was about not wallowing in the past, but getting on with it and having hope for the future. It wasn't a religion or anything, but I think Jane would have approved.

Scott didn't talk on the phone too much, like he said, but we texted a lot. Pretty much every day. When my eyes got tired and I couldn't read or write anymore, I played checkers or pool with Barry. He always beat me at checkers and I always beat him at pool. I felt bad about the things I'd thought about Barry when I first got to Carville, because he was actually a real sweetheart. Socially awkward as hell, but sweet. He knew a lot about space and stars and planets and asteroids, that type of stuff. He would always let me know what was going to happen that night in the sky. He called them "celestial events." It made me feel like I was invited to a fancy party. One day when we were playing pool, I told Barry about the book I was working on, my story.

"Sounds interesting," he said.

"I don't know if anyone would ever want to read it, or if I could get it published or whatever, but . . . I think I'd like to try." I took my shot. The six ball bounced off the corner. Nothing went down.

Barry looked at me, waiting for more.

"I found something I actually really like to do. And I think . . . I mean, I hope, I might even be good at it. Or at least not totally suck at it."

"Writing?"

I nodded.

"Like, books?"

"Yeah, I mean, I know I'll have to work on it for a few years, and it's not like I know the first thing about how to become a professional writer or what to do when I actually finish it, but, that's the cool thing, I *want* to work on it. Even if nothing happens. I mean, if it never gets published or whatever. That's, like, not the point. The writing *itself* is the point."

Barry nodded slowly.

"Does that make sense?"

"Yes," Barry said. He gazed out the window. "I have a cousin," Barry said. He took the square of chalk from the edge of the table and ground it into the tip of his cue. He studied me without looking at me. His bug eyes flicking around my hair, my jeans.

"Yeah . . . ?"

"Yeah." Barry set down the chalk and lined up his shot. The ball went in. He lined up for the next shot. He held his tongue between his teeth, concentrating.

I waited.

He missed.

I lined up and sunk the six in the side pocket. "So what about your cousin?" I said.

"Oh, yeah, well." He pushed his glasses up on his nose. "She teaches in the creative writing department at Columbia. Maybe she could give you some tips. Point you in the right direction."

"Columbia. That's in New York, right?"

"Yes."

I thought of Jane's theory about the two kinds of people. Maybe I was a New York person after all.

"If you want, I could ask her to take a look at your book. Once you've finished it and everything."

"Seriously? You'd do that for me?"

"Sure." He shrugged. "Why not?"

I took my shot. The seven rocketed into the corner pocket. "That would be awesome," I said. I smiled at him and shot my next ball. The five went into the side pocket with a clatter.

"I, for one, can't wait to read it," he said.

"Thanks, Barry." I gently tapped the eight ball into the side pocket and won the game.

"Here, I'll give you my email. And I'll get in touch with my cousin and let her know you'll be contacting her." He took a pencil and a scrap of paper out of his breast pocket and wrote his email address out. He handed me the paper.

And just like that, I had a plan B. I looked up at Barry, blinking in the light. He smiled sheepishly, scratched the stubble on his chin. I knew that once I left Carville, I wouldn't be able to judge people based on their looks anymore. I'd learned too much.

I worked hard at my physical therapy and made sure I was getting lots of rest and good nutrition; I kept writing in my red notebooks, going for walks around the lake, reading, doing schoolwork. I hung out with Barry quite a bit and had tea and cookies with Grace and Lester every Saturday, and then one day, it was my last day at Carville and I was allowed to go home—for good.

The week I got home, I got a letter from my school that pretty much said that if I wrote my final exams, I was going to pass twelfth grade and I was in good shape to be on the honor roll. Even though I had missed so much school, I had still, inexplicably, done very well. Maybe even better than I would have if I had actually been attending school, since I didn't get distracted by all the high school drama. I mean, the letter didn't say that last part, but that's what I figured. I put the letter down on the table and breathed a sigh of relief. I would tell Mom and Dad when they got home from work and they would be so happy. The sunlight blasted through the kitchen windows and our house was quiet and bright. In a few weeks, I would be walking across the stage to accept a diploma at my graduation ceremony, and, if I wanted to, going to prom.

My heart fluttered. I didn't want to think about it for too long because I didn't want to chicken out. I fired off a text to Scott: Will you go to my prom with me?

I held my phone and my breath, watching the ellipses appear as he typed his reply.

As long as I don't have to wear a baby-blue tux.

I laughed. Typed: You can wear whatever you want.

In the weeks leading up to my prom, Scott and I devised an elaborate plan. He would buy (not steal—buy) a car, or maybe a van, with the money he had saved up from his job working construction. Then he would drive down to Texas, come with me to prom, and we would leave the next day to visit Dean and Kyle in San Francisco. We'd take a few days to do the drive, take in the sights, camp along the way, or maybe sleep in the car, depending on what kind of car he got. I was so excited I could barely sleep at night. I studied maps and roadside diners on the Internet and vaguely wondered if I would lose my (born-again) virginity somewhere along the side of the road in California.

Mom took me shopping for my prom dress and I chose a coral cut-out dress that came to just above the ankle. Coral because, let's face it, everyone looks good in coral, especially blondes. Cut-out because Jane had said that style would look good on me and, turns out, she was right. It was really elegant; it showed off my neckline and collarbones so I had to find the perfect jewelry to go with it.

With Dean gone, the house was eerily quiet, and it seemed to stay clean and tidy all on its own. I went in to school to write my final exams but didn't go back for classes. I didn't really see the point. I worked on my book instead.

Although Mom and Dad would never admit it, I think they really missed Dean. And I would never tell him this in a million years, but so did I.

Dad didn't seem to know what to do with himself. He was spending a lot of time in the garage. Fiddling with things and fixing things that didn't necessarily need to be fixed. One night I went out to the garage to visit him. I clutched the gold armadillo coin in my fist.

"Hey, Dad. How's it going out here?"

"Oh, hi, Abby." He looked up from his workbench where he was gluing a broken picture frame together. "What's up?"

"I was wondering if you would be able to make a hole in this." I held out the coin.

He took it from me and turned it over and over in the palm of his hand. "This is pretty neat, hey?"

"Yeah."

"Did you get this from . . . ?"

I nodded.

"Yeah, I should be able to drill a hole through it, no problem."

"Cool. How long do you think it will take?"

He stood up. "I can do it right now."

I watched as he put the coin in his vise and clamped it, then got out his drill and turned it on. The metal shrieked as he drilled into it, but then it was done, it was over. He took the coin out and blew on it, then handed it back to me, smiling. "There you go, sweetie."

The coin was hot in my hand. I held it up to examine the hole winking in the center of the armadillo.

Scott and I didn't take a limo to prom or anything fancy like that. We drove in the van he had bought two days before, a 1962 Volkswagen camper van, eggplant purple, that he had bought off a couple of hippies for a song.

"It'll be perfect for our trip!" he said, as he showed me the van. "Look at all this room!"

I had to admit, the van was pretty sweet. It even had little tie-dye curtains and matching pillows that someone had made especially for it. There was a tiny sink and a mini-fridge in the back. There was a table built into the side that you could flip up into the wall when you wanted more room. "Look," Scott said, putting the table down. "We can sit here and play cards." He grinned.

My mom was smitten over the van, and maybe with Scott a little, too. His hair had gotten longer, and he had gotten stronger and leaner working construction in the months since he'd left Louisiana.

"I would have *loved* something like this when I was your age," Mom gushed, running her hand over a headlight. "You're so lucky, Abby. You're going to have such a great trip. What an adventure!"

So we arrived in style to the prom. Scott wore dark jeans, a white dress shirt and a black pin-stripe jacket. He parked the van and I sat quietly in the passenger seat with my hands in my lap.

"You ready for this?" he said.

I grabbed onto my left hand to stop it from shaking. "I guess I'm a little nervous," I said. "It's been a while since I've been around all these people and . . . things are so different now. *I'm* different."

"You want to bail and just keep driving? Because we could do that."

I breathed in. Breathed out. "No," I said. "I want to do this."

"Okay then," Scott said. "Let's do this!" He got out and slammed his door, then came around to my side and opened the door for me and helped me out. "And did I mention how absolutely fabulous you look tonight, Miss Furlowe?"

I laughed. "Thanks. You're looking pretty fabulous yourself."

"Well, I did comb my hair for the occasion."

I laughed.

"Oh no! Wait! I almost forgot. Hang on." He unlocked the van and climbed into the back. I could see him through the windows, getting something out of the mini-fridge.

I took my compact out of my purse and checked my makeup. "Okay," I said under my breath. "You're okay." When Scott came back, I clicked my compact shut and slid it back into my purse.

"Here," he said. "Give me your wrist." He held a wrist corsage with a white magnolia in the center of it.

"Oh my goodness," I said. "Thank you! It's beautiful."

He carefully fastened it around my wrist. "My mom helped me pick it out," he said, shrugging.

"Aw, that's so cute," I said. "I really like it."

"I'm glad."

I admired the corsage, breathing in its scent. "It reminds me of the magnolias at Carville."

"Me too," he said. Then he offered me his arm. "Shall we?"

I took his arm and we went into the banquet hall.

We had time to cruise around for a while before the dinner started. The dance followed the dinner and then they would announce the prom king and queen. We got some punch and I hoped that someone had spiked it.

Everyone was dressed to the nines. It was pretty cool checking everyone out. Some people cleaned up so well I barely recognized them. Dustin came over and said hi. Aaron came over and said hi. Marla ran up to us while we were on our second round at the punch table. "Oh my God, Abby?!" She wore an emerald green tea-length dress and had her hair in an up-do. She squealed, hugged me. "Abby you look *so good*!"

"Thanks," I said. "I feel good. That's the important part." I glanced at Scott. He smiled at me. I introduced them. I could tell Marla thought he was hot. Obviously.

"Where's Liz?" I said.

Marla shook her head. "Nate doesn't do prom. You know . . . so . . . she didn't come."

"That's too bad," I said. "She's only been talking about it for three years."

"Yeah, well," Marla said. "She'll regret it. One day."

Marla leaned closer to me. "I love your necklace," she said. "Is that an armadillo?"

"Yeah," I said.

"So cool! Where did you get it?"

"Well," I said, glancing at Scott. "It's kind of a long story."

She nodded. Took a sip of her punch. "We probably have a few minutes before dinner starts," she said.

"Maybe some other time," I said.

"Oh. Okay, well . . . I should check on my date, I guess," she said, glancing behind her. "It was so good to see you, Abby. You look so great. You really do."

"Thanks."

"And nice to meet you, Scott."

"Likewise," he said.

She gave us a little wave and went away.

"Friend of yours?" Scott said.

"Best friend," I said. "Used to be."

"She doesn't know, does she?"

"Nope."

"Are you going to tell her ever, do you think?"

"I don't know," I said. "Maybe I'll just send her a copy of my book instead."

"A signed copy," he said.

I shrugged. "If she's lucky."

"Whew! Don't mess with Texas!" He laughed.

Then they made the announcement that dinner was about to be served and we made our way back to our table and sat down. The other people at our table came to take their seats. I said hello to them. Scott took my hand and held it on his knee. I gazed out over the balloons and streamers and sparkly decorations. I knew that I wasn't going to be crowned prom queen, and I didn't care one bit. I was happy.

Author's Note

I want to apologize for using the words *leper* and *leprosy* to those who are offended by these terms. Most people who have been affected by leprosy (now called Hansen's disease) find the word *leper* derogatory, as it defines individuals solely based on their disease and carries over two thousand years of stigma with it. Many people have advocated for the name to be changed to Hansen's disease, after the Norwegian scientist Dr. Gerhard H.A. Hansen who first discovered the bacteria in 1873. In some countries, including Brazil and Japan, the name has been officially changed.

I have nothing but respect and admiration for those individuals who have suffered or are suffering from Hansen's disease, and I hope they will forgive me for using "the L-word" for the purpose of telling this story authentically in Abby's voice.

Further, I would like to acknowledge that Hansen's disease *has* naturally occurred in animals other than the nine-banded armadillo, including the African chimpanzee, sooty mangabey monkeys, the cynomolgus macaque and red squirrels.

For more information about Hansen's disease:
www.idealeprosydignity.org (International)
www.effecthope.org (Canada)
www.leprosy.org (United States)
www.nippon-foundation.or.jp (Japan)

THANK YOU

My first reader, Ben Parker: I don't know what I would do without you. My agent, Hilary McMahon, head cheerleader for this book. Lynne Missen and my editor, Samantha Swenson, for seeing Abby's potential and helping me to realize it. Mitch Glessing for the jokes. My student at the Humber School for Writers, Abby Birmingham, who reminded me of the power of voice and whose character, "Faith," inspired me to create Abby. Lorna Jackson, who assigned a historical fiction research project to our workshop in 2002 which led me to discover British Columbia's lazaretto, D'Arcy Island, and inspired further research on its inhabitants and Hansen's disease patients worldwide. Jacqueline Beamish, thank you for your assistance with my research and sending me the information I requested on leprosy in the Bible. My parents, Jennifer Little and John Little, who I know would show up early on visitor's day. And thank you Warren Sookocheff for your unending patience, love and support.

The Canada Council for the Arts and the Access Copyright Foundation provided financial assistance in support of this book. The Vancouver Public Library's Writer in Residence program and Wilfrid Laurier University's Edna Staebler Writer in Residence program provided financial assistance and time to write this novel. I am grateful to these institutions.

In my research I consulted the memoirs of former Carville residents Betty White, Stanley Stein, José P. Ramirez and Neil White, as well as an ethnography by Dr. Marcia Gaudet. I am thankful for their work.